"You're afraid I'll make a pass, right?"

Jack asked, raising a speculative brow.

Tess shook her head too vehemently. "No, I'm not."

Innocence filled his eyes. "Oh, then you're worried *you* might make one?"

"No," she replied. "I have work to do. You hired me to teach you wilderness skills, not to be your personal attendant."

"You're right," he said contritely. "But would you mind if I did?"

"Did what?"

"Make a pass at you."

"Yes. But get it over with, for Pete's sake, so I can push you away and tell you there can be nothing between us but business," she told him in exasperation. "It'll save time all around."

"I don't believe you," he said, catching her wrist in his hand. "When I touch you, I get a whole different message...."

Dear Reader,

Summer romance . . . does anything tug at the heartstrings more? We've all experienced poignant first love at a vacation resort or those balmy summer nights on the porch swing with that special man—if not in real life, then certainly in the pages of Silhouette Romance novels, the perfect summertime reading!

This month, our heroines find their heroes around the world—in Mexico, Italy, Australia—*and* right in their own backyard. And what heroes they find, from the mysterious stranger to the charming man of their dreams!

July continues our WRITTEN IN THE STARS series. Each month in 1991, we're proud to present a book that focuses on the hero—and his astrological sign. July features the passionate, possessive and vulnerable Cancerian man in Val Whisenand's *For Eternity*.

Silhouette Romance novels *always* reflect the magic of love in heartwarming stories that will make you laugh and cry and move you time and time again. In the months to come, watch for books by your all-time favorites, including Diana Palmer, Brittany Young, Annette Broadrick and many others.

I hope you enjoy this book and all our future Silhouette Romance stories. We'd love to hear from you!

Sincerely,

Valerie Susan Hayward
Senior Editor

PEPPER ADAMS

Hunter At Large

Published by Silhouette Books New York

America's Publisher of Contemporary Romance

We dedicate this book to the outdoor enthusiasts of
the world and to those who are not so enthusiastic
about the great outdoors. We take this opportunity
to thank those who answered our many, many
questions and made it possible to write
Hunter At Large.

SILHOUETTE BOOKS
300 E. 42nd St., New York, N.Y. 10017

HUNTER AT LARGE

ISBN: 0-373-08805-1

First Silhouette Books printing July 1991

All the characters in this book have no existence
outside the imagination of the author and have
no relation whatsoever to anyone bearing the same
name or names. They are not even distantly
inspired by any individual known or unknown
to the author, and all incidents are pure invention.

®: Trademark used under license and
registered in the United States Patent and
Trademark Office and in other countries.

Printed in the U.S.A.

PEPPER ADAMS

lives in Oklahoma with her husband and children. Her interest in romance writing began with obsessive reading and was followed by writing courses, where she learned the craft. She longs for the discipline of the "rigid schedule" all the how-to books exhort writers to maintain, but does not seriously believe she will achieve one in this lifetime. She finds she works best if she remembers to take her writing, and not herself, seriously.

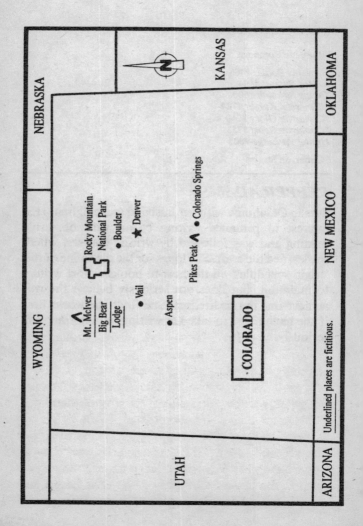

WYOMING

NEBRASKA

UTAH

Mt. McIver

Rocky Mountain
National Park

Big Bear
Lodge

● Boulder

★ Denver

● Vail

● Aspen

Pikes Peak ● Colorado Springs

COLORADO

KANSAS

N

ARIZONA

NEW MEXICO

OKLAHOMA

Underlined places are fictitious.

Chapter One

"What do you mean he's already here?" Tess McIver was beginning to dislike Jack Hunter, and she hadn't even met the man yet.

"Now don't act like you was raised on sour milk," her father, Bitterroot, admonished. "He showed up whilst you were in town gettin' supplies and I sent him on up to his cabin." Twenty-four years of dealing with his headstrong daughter's many moods had served the old man well. "He's waitin' to talk to you."

"Well, he can just wait," she dismissed. "Today's Friday. He wasn't supposed to arrive until Monday."

"I know it. But he's chompin' at the bit."

Bitterroot's satisfied chuckle made Tess focus her frustration on him. "If I didn't know better, I'd swear you broke your danged foot on purpose." She paced around the pine-paneled lobby of Big Bear Lodge, her hands jammed deep in the pockets of her denim pants.

The determined ring of her boot heels on the oak floor was a fair indication of her agitation.

''Now, why in tarnation would I go and do a fool thing like that?'' Bitterroot's indignation was that of an affronted banty rooster.

Tess eyed her father. The innocent expression on his grizzled face was supposed to make her feel guilty for snapping at him. It didn't. ''Contrariness?''

''Contrary? Me?'' the old man sputtered. ''That's fine talk comin' from a gal who could write a book on the subject.'' Shifting his meager weight in his favorite old chair, he rearranged his cast on a threadbare ottoman and winced as pain ricocheted through his foot.

Tess was at his side immediately. ''Let me help you, Pop.''

He swatted her away. ''Quit treating me like a sick kitten. Why, a man would have to be loco to throw himself on your mercy.''

She backed off to give her father the independence he needed, but she didn't back down. ''You knew I was opposed to Jack Hunter coming here. It was pretty inconsiderate of you to fall through the roof and dump him in my lap.''

Opposed was putting it mildly. She'd been furious when she'd heard about her father's plan to bail the lodge out of financial trouble.

''Well, excuse me for living, missy.'' Bitterroot folded his arms across his chest and glared at her from under bushy brows. His snow-white hair was furrowed with comb tracks, and his bristly mustache twitched. "It was pretty damned inconsiderate of that roof to cave in, if you ask me."

Tess softened. He was lucky to have only broken a couple of metatarsal bones in the fall. She was happy to have him yelling at her, irascible as ever. He was still a scurrilous old coot, but he was *her* scurrilous old coot. They'd always been close, but since her mother's death ten years ago, the two had become more than father and daughter; they'd become friends. Over the years they had disagreed on just about everything, but never as vehemently as this.

It had started when a local television celebrity approached Bitterroot with a business proposition. Jack Hunter wanted the best wilderness guide in Colorado to turn him into a "true" sportsman. He was willing to pay handsomely for one-on-one lessons, providing they wouldn't take more than thirty days of his precious time.

Tess's first response had been to ask why the host of Denver's most popular outdoor program needed wilderness training in the first place. Bitterroot had relayed the story as Hunter had told it to him. Six months ago, the former star had walked out when the producers refused to meet his salary demands. Jack Hunter, a writer for the show, had been recruited as a temporary replacement.

However, audience response to the new host was so favorable that the ratings-hungry producers had changed the name of the program to *Hunter At Large* and signed Hunter to a lengthy contract. It was a show business Cinderella story, with one minor hitch; the star, by his own admission, wasn't the almighty guru of the great outdoors he appeared to be on-screen.

He claimed he'd planned all along to get the training but there hadn't been time until now. Tess suspected Hunter was afraid his fans would find out he was really just a know-nothing greenhorn who was fed information via a weekly script. He'd look pretty foolish if that happened, and that's why he'd appealed to Bitterroot for help.

Bitterroot had jumped at the chance to make some money during the month the lodge was normally closed to visitors. Now that he was sidelined with an injury, it was up to Tess to help Hunter pass muster. If she refused, he risked being revealed as a fraud, and worse, Big Bear Lodge would have to do without badly needed repairs.

"I'm a reasonable woman." Tess ignored Bitterroot's derisive snort. "I agreed to take your place because I know how much we need the money. But I don't have to like it." She made no mention of her own responsibility for their financial ills; by tacit agreement that sore subject had been closed to discussion three years ago.

"Do you think I took a nosedive through the roof to make a point or to get out of baby-sitting duty?" her father huffed.

"Neither." Tess felt properly chastised. "It's just that it goes against my principles to help Hunter. He's nothing but a phony." And she'd had enough dealings with phonies to last a lifetime.

"Tarnation, gal, ease up on the poor fella. If he didn't have good intentions he wouldn't be here."

Bitterroot scratched around his cast with a pencil. "Look at it this way, he's a-tryin' to do the right thing."

"He's trying to save his a—"

"Tess McIver! I know I let you grow up wild and unfettered in these woods, but it ain't ladylike to talk thataway."

"Then I guess I'm not a lady." She spun on her heel and headed for the door. She had no desire to confront Hunter in her current mood. But since he was here she'd have to do it sooner or later, and Tess never shirked unpleasant tasks. "I'll go talk to the man."

"Thatagirl," Bitterroot called after her. "He ain't a bad sort. He's city bred, that's for sure, and he's slicker than calf-slobber, but nothin' you can't handle. He's ready, willin', and looked plenty able enough to me. Said he hopes to get started right away. Maybe even this evenin'."

"We'll start Monday as agreed. A deal's a deal." A code of honor could be a real pain, Tess mused. On her way out the door, she patted the massive stuffed grizzly bear that had given the lodge its name. Woodrow, as he'd been dubbed, had been bagged by her great-grandfather. Aside from her father, Woodrow was one of the few reliable males she knew. However, as Tess flounced out for her meeting with the notorious Jack Hunter, it seemed to her that even Woodrow had a smug look on his bearish face.

Her great-grandfather Josiah McIver, the son of an early settler, had started the hunting lodge when this part of the Rock was little more than a wilderness. The small town of Big Bear had grown up around it in the ensuing years. Only a few hundred hardy souls called it home permanently, but it boasted a fair-size seasonal population.

Cradled high in the Rocky Mountains eighty miles northwest of Denver, the Big Bear area was a sportsman's paradise. The forests teemed with game, and the lakes and streams were filled with pike and trout. Abundant snowfall attracted winter sports enthusiasts to nearby recreation areas. In the summer, campers and hikers were lured by the unspoiled beauty of the wilderness.

As one of the oldest and most respected lodges and outfitters in the state, the McIvers' business should have been thriving. In truth, they were barely hanging on while they tried to pay off a mortgage that never would have existed if Tess had used better sense.

She acknowledged that she might have been taken in once by a good-looking, smooth-talking man, but as sure as a buck goes barefoot, she wouldn't be fooled again.

Walking down the well-worn path from the lodge to the little guest cabins, she observed that if it wasn't for men, her life would be much less complicated. Her thoughts turned to Greg Dexter as they often did when she was in a disparaging mood, and she cursed him. Not so much for the emotional pain he'd caused her, but for the lasting fiscal damage he'd done the lodge.

Her tender young heart had mended, but her bank account still suffered from his duplicity. She'd been unable to replace the money Greg had stolen, but she'd learned to keep her emotions safe within a shell of distrust, a shell that should have been too hard for a twenty-four-year-old woman to maintain. Except for her father, Tess didn't take any man seriously. And after what Bitterroot had gotten her into with Jack Hunter, maybe she would reserve judgment on him as well.

Halfway to the clearing where the ten ramshackle guest cabins stood, Tess perched on a stump to enjoy a moment of quiet. The soothing magic of the forest was just what she needed before she confronted Hunter.

She watched a fat squirrel scrabble down a pine tree a few yards away. It was the middle of August, and the little fellow was scurrying around, gathering food for the hard winter to come. Since the first snow sometimes fell as early as Labor Day in the mountains, he was no doubt feeling pressured to hurry.

The sun hung in the sky just above the tall evergreens, reluctant to give up its hold on the day. When it dropped behind the trees, darkness would come quickly, but now the cool shadows of the ponderosa pines and Douglas firs made a lacy design on the needle-carpeted ground. Tess drew a deep breath, enjoying the sweet resinous fragrance of the woods.

The only sounds were the soft soughing of the wind in the trees and the call of a nearby junco. She closed her eyes, and as always when she was outdoors, she felt her worries and troubles slip away. Fresh air and freedom restored her in a way nothing else could. She considered herself lucky to belong to the land. Four generations of McIvers had struggled and loved and lived on this soil; she wasn't about to be the one who lost it.

Suddenly the quiet twilight was rent by an unexpected explosion. Tess jumped to her feet and the startled squirrel disappeared up a tree. The thunderous blast echoed for a long moment, but she immediately recognized it for what it was.

Gunfire!

The shot had come from Cabin Ten, a couple of hundred yards deeper in the woods. The structure crouched in the gathering gloom of evening, a dark shape draped in darker shadows. Before Tess could move in that direction, a man appeared in the doorway of the isolated cabin.

"Help me," he called in a choked voice. "I've shot my damn leg off."

He crumpled to the ground and Tess bolted for the cabin. He was still conscious when she reached him, his face pale and contorted with pain. He moaned when she rolled him gently onto his back. Grasping his upper left thigh with both hands, he muttered, "Damn thing went off! Just like that, it went off!"

In the quiet forest, the gunshot had sounded like a cannon blast, and Tess expected to find an ugly gaping hole, furious with blood and black with powder burn. Looking the man over quickly, she was darned if she could find any sign of damage.

"Where's the wound?" she demanded.

"Here," he moaned.

"Here where?"

"Here *here*," Jack Hunter grunted ungraciously. "My leg." He couldn't believe he'd shot himself. He knew all about guns and gun safety, in theory and in philosophy. He had his friend Norton Greene to thank for that. But all that book learning had not prepared him for this reality.

How would he explain this? An accident like this could ruin him in more ways than one.

The rapidly descending darkness frustrated Tess's efforts to examine Hunter's injury. "I can't see anything. I need to get you into the cabin where the light's better. Can you stand?"

"You're kidding," he answered crossly. "Only an idiot would ask a man with a bullet hole in his leg if he can stand."

"Well then, can you hobble, crawl or drag yourself on your belly?" Tess had already decided not to like Jack Hunter, and her impatience with his attitude made her curt. "I can't carry a big lug like you, and it's getting dark fast out here."

"I'll try." To Jack's surprise, he'd felt very little pain for the first few minutes. That was no longer true. His leg hurt like hell. He managed to get to his feet and, with his arm across the woman's shoulders, limped into the cabin.

Tess half dragged him inside and led him to the bed where he collapsed in a groaning heap. When she pried his hands off his leg she saw the powder burn on his jeans. After his melodramatic display, she was amazed that the bullet had made such a small hole and had resulted in so little blood loss. The wound was high on the inside of his left thigh, and she had to wonder how he'd managed to shoot himself in that particular spot.

As gently as she could, she lifted his leg and looked at the other side. The powder burn was larger and there was more blood at the point of exit. She couldn't help grimacing when she examined the injury.

"Be careful, dammit!" Jack snapped.

Ignoring his churlish behavior, she expressed her dismay with a low, speculative whistle.

"What?" he asked, his voice tinged with panic. "Is it bad?"

"I don't think so."

"When do you think you'll know?" he asked sarcastically.

"I can barely see it. I realize that in the movies it's standard procedure to rip off pant legs with the teeth, but given the delicate location of your wound and the durability of Levi's, I suggest you remove your jeans the conventional way." She clamped her hands on her hips and waited.

"Can't we just call 911?" he asked.

"Out here, I'm the closest thing to it. So, shuck those pants."

Jack wasn't sure who this angel of unmercy was, but it was obvious she meant business. With the lodge closed for repairs, Bitterroot McIver had promised there would be no other guests during the month he was booked. Then he'd arrived and found his erstwhile teacher in a cast.

Bitterroot had told him not to worry, his partner would take over. He'd assumed the partner was another grizzled old mountain man, but given his luck lately it was probably Paula Bunyan here.

Jack tried to bring her face into focus but the pain made it swim in front of him. "If you want my pants off, lady, you'll have to do it yourself. I'm in no condition.''

Tess took a close look at the man for the first time. Not that she hadn't seen him before. She'd been suckered into watching his stupid show often enough. It was easy to see why Jack Hunter was such a success in a medium where appearance was more important than integrity.

He was lumberjack tall, brawny but not beefy. He had narrow hips and wide shoulders made for down vests and flannel shirts. His dark brown hair was thick and wavy and was probably very photogenic blowing in a soft breeze off a lake. His handsome face was all sculpted chin and cheekbones, and his brown eyes, though slightly glazed at the moment, would no doubt be intense under better circumstances. Although it was drawn into a grimace of pain, his generous mouth was unmistakably sensual.

She estimated that he was a few years older than her own twenty-four years, and though rugged was the technical term for his looks, hunk was the popular expression. He was the type some women got into cat fights over. But not Tess McIver.

Her scrutiny was too obvious, and while he was in no position to make demands, Jack demanded, "Are you going to stand there gaping while I suffer? Go to the lodge and get Bitterroot's partner."

Tess tried to ignore Hunter's tone. "I *am* his partner. I'm also his daughter. My name's Tess McIver."

Jack didn't have a chance to discuss that unexpected revelation. With the deftness of a skilled orderly, Tess flipped him onto his back, tugged off his

boots and stripped off his tight jeans as if she un-
dressed men every day. In the process, her hand un-
avoidably slid down the inside of his muscular thigh,
but as far as he could tell, she didn't seem to notice.

Despite the bombardment of her senses by blatant
virility, Tess achieved just the right note of indifference and sarcasm. "Since the nearest hospital is more
than forty miles away, I think I should administer
some first aid before we call for help."

"Are you qualified to do that?" he asked skeptically.

"I'm no combat doctor, but I've seen my share of
hunting accidents. I think I can keep you alive until the
medics arrive."

"Forget it. You can't call an ambulance." As soon
as he realized he wasn't going to die, Jack knew he
didn't want any more people than necessary to find
out about this.

"Why not? Are you worried the attendants might
ask embarrassing questions?"

The answering profanity rang with the derision
usually reserved for perpetrators of crimes against
man and God.

"What an attitude," she muttered. "Maybe you'd
rather be left alone to suffer this great agony in silence." She turned away, but he grabbed her arm.

"No, please. I'm sorry. Do something, I don't want
to bleed to death." What an ignominious end that
would be, Jack thought between surges of pain. The
famous Jack Hunter, felled by his own hand.

"There's little chance of that happening." Having
divested the victim of his pants, Tess examined the

wound as carefully as she could, considering the location. She tried to keep her eyes on the injury and off the anatomy. The bullet had passed cleanly through the flesh. The skin surrounding the small entry hole was not badly damaged or too ragged for a doctor to repair.

She gave him an on-the-spot prognosis. "You're lucky. We won't have to send for a priest after all, and I can almost guarantee that amputation won't be necessary. Skill alone doesn't account for how you did it, but you managed to miss both the bone and the artery. As they say in the movies, it's only a flesh wound."

"*Only* a flesh wound, she says." Jack flopped back on the bed and beseeched heaven for the strength he felt ebbing away.

"You'll need stitches, and the wound might require draining. I'll go to the lodge and phone for an ambulance. Or would a big star like yourself prefer a limousine to take you to the hospital in style?"

"You're not calling anyone." Jack clutched her hand before she could leave his side. "I can't let this news out. You aren't getting out of my sight."

She perched on the bedside chair. "Then I may as well make myself comfortable."

"Forgive me if I'm not particularly concerned about your comfort at the moment."

"I imagine you're too worried about what all your fans are going to think of the great white hunter."

Jack groaned and clutched her hand. "Give me a break, lady. Look, you said you had experience with things like this. Can't you just clean it out and sew me up?'' He shuddered at the thought, but it was better than having to explain the wound to a hospital staff.

''I said I'd seen hunting accidents. Most of those occur when hunters fall out of the trees they climb to get the drop on unsuspecting game.'' She managed to conceal her smile. ''I'm in no position to sew you up. Since I didn't know Billy the Kid was coming, I didn't stock up on sterile sutures.''

''What did they do before sterile sutures were invented?''

''I believe they died from lockjaw and infection,'' she stated dryly. ''I guess if I can find a needle and thread in my pocket, all we need is a little whiskey for anesthetic and we're in business.''

Jack frowned and actually considered her suggestion for a moment.

''I was joking. You don't want to submit to anything that primitive.'' He still held her hand and she didn't care for the feelings his touch aroused. They were even more intense than the ones that had gotten her in trouble with the odious Greg Dexter.

Jack captured her blue gaze with his dark brown one and held it. ''Believe me, I'm feeling particularly primitive right now. The whiskey's on the dresser.''

Ignoring his husky comments, she pulled her hand out of his and went on seriously. ''This needs more attention than you might think. You'll need a tetanus shot and antibiotic to prevent infection.''

''I had a tetanus shot before I came,'' he insisted.

''Oh?'' She quirked an untamed auburn brow in his direction. ''Do you have a history of self-inflicted violence?''

"No, I do not have a history of self-inflicted violence," he mimicked through clenched teeth. He was striving to remain calm, but the woman's sarcasm was infuriating.

"Then how do you feel about gangrene?"

"Are you always so sensitive and understanding?" he asked.

"I won't waste any more patience on the likes of you." She turned away from him and went into the bathroom. She came back with a damp washcloth and placed it over the wound. "Here, press down on this. I guess even you deserve medical attention. Put your pants on and I'll drive you to the hospital. It'll be faster than waiting for the ambulance."

"Hospital?" He hated the idea. "How about an old country doctor?"

"None around here."

"Have you no consideration for a man's last request?"

She laughed but she didn't sound amused. "Believe me fella, you'll live to request again."

Realizing what a grouch he'd been, he looked down at his thigh and marveled all over again how close he'd come to unmanning himself. "But will I enjoy it?"

She shrugged. "I don't see why not. You didn't hit anything vital."

"In that case, maybe I should take my chances with gangrene."

"No way. Now will you come along quietly or do I have to scare up a posse?"

"I'll go peaceably." He sighed and gave up trying to change her mind. She was a strong-willed woman, and he was too smart to risk infection. "Can I have a little of that frontier painkiller before we leave?" He gestured at the whiskey bottle on the nightstand.

"I don't think you should."

"Well I do," he snapped crossly.

"Not exactly a happy camper, are you?"

"Given the dire nature of my injury, I figure I'm entitled to a little pique."

"It's your funeral." She picked up the bottle and examined the label. At his reproachful look, she added, "Sorry for the poor choice of words." She smirked as she handed him the whiskey. "I see there's a picture of a turkey on the label. How appropriate."

He made a face at her and took a hearty swallow, but the fiery liquid burned as much as the pain in his leg. "I'm ready when you are."

"You're forgetting something." Tess handed him his jeans and watched him take another long gulp of whiskey before averting her gaze. His eyes watered and his face reddened with the effort not to choke. Obviously Jack Hunter did not habitually drink whiskey straight from the bottle.

He plunked it down and gingerly worked his injured leg into his pants. Tess turned her back on him. There was no point in dwelling on the superb degree to which his buns filled out his baby-blue, barely-there briefs.

Chapter Two

Displaying what Jack considered amazing strength and efficiency, Tess helped him into his car. After a brief stop at the lodge to tell Bitterroot their destination, she pulled the sporty Mercedes-Benz onto the road to Vail, the nearest town with a hospital.

Handling the car's high-tech controls with surprising skill, Tess gave Jack a curious look and asked the question she'd obviously been dying to ask. "How about telling me what happened?"

"Before I do, you have to promise you won't tell anyone else. Ever!"

"I'm in no position to make empty promises. I'm still a tad unnerved."

Now that the painkiller had kicked in, Jack could spare his personal good Samaritan some attention. He wondered if she was being sarcastic again. The woman beside him was the picture of rock-steady calm and self-assured competence. He doubted if she'd be un-nerved by the sight of a UFO off-loading little green men.

She was tall and generously proportioned in the sleekly muscled way of serious athletes. Even the mannish clothes she wore—denim pants, chambray work skirt and cowboy boots—couldn't disguise the lushness of her curves. Her shoulder-length hair was the deep auburn of a fall maple leaf and was pulled back into a sleek ponytail, worn with a fringe of bangs.

Her blue eyes were disarming in their directness, and her firm chin had a stubborn slant to it. Even her soft, kissable mouth was set in a determined line, as though she didn't often allow it to lapse into a smile.

She was nothing like the women who usually appealed to Jack. Those soft helpless little creatures clung admiringly to his every word, while Tess McIver appeared immune to the charm that had served him in the past. Still, her warrior-maiden mystique was riveting in its way.

"Something tells me," he said when he'd finished his assessment, "that very little unnerves you."

"True. But I'm not often called upon to help a person with a self-inflicted gunshot wound."

"Will you please stop referring to it like that?" He didn't even try to hide his exasperation. "You make it sound like a suicide attempt."

She looked at him quickly. "Was it?"

"Of course not. If I'd wanted to blow my brains out, don't you think I would have aimed a little higher?"

"I don't know." She shrugged and returned her eyes to the winding mountain road. "I guess it depends on the location of your particular brains. You could just be a lousy shot, for all I know."

"I am, but take my word for it, it was an accident. I'm perfectly knowledgeable about gun safety, and I thought I had the situation under control. I simply made a mistake."

Tess's condescending harrumph prompted Jack to unwilling defensiveness. "Of course that's a concept that you, in all your perfection, probably do not understand."

His peevish tone almost elicited a smile, but Tess got it under control in time. "Oh, I understand mistakes all right." With a pointed glance in his direction, she added, "I've made one or two myself."

He opted to let the comment pass. "Unfortunately people in my position aren't supposed to make those kind of errors. If word of this leaks out, I'll be laughed out of the business."

"Maybe you should be."

"What do you mean by that?"

"Nothing," she said evasively.

"Can you understand why I don't want the world to know about this . . . er . . . a—"

"Error?" Tess finished for him.

"Accident," he insisted.

She finally gave in to the urge to laugh. "Yeah, I have a pretty fair idea."

The unexpectedness of her laugh disarmed Jack. It was rich and feminine and seductive. And it restored his usually high spirits enough to let him join her.

"Must you have so much fun at my expense? It's very hard on my ego."

"Sorry. So how did you do it?"

"Do what?"

"Come close to being the only self-made eunuch on television."

Jack didn't appreciate her choice of words. "I was loading the clip into my pistol and it jammed. When I couldn't get it in, I—"

"Braced it against your leg?" she guessed.

"That's right."

"No, that's wrong."

"Yeah, well you know what they say about hindsight," he snapped. This line of questioning made him uncomfortable, so he changed the subject. "You can imagine my surprise when you showed up. Bitterroot neglected to mention that his partner was a woman."

"Pop does enjoy his little jokes," she admitted wryly. "I hope my gender won't affect our relationship."

He feigned surprise. "Are we going to have one?"

"Our *working* relationship," she stressed. "Next to Pop, I'm the best guide in this part of the country. I've lived here all my life, and I know the wilderness and how to survive in it. I'm a crack shot as well as a skilled angler, and I can teach you everything you need to know."

"I don't doubt it for a minute, but maybe I can teach you a few things as well," he said in his best preseduction voice.

Tess looked down her magnificent nose at him. "I want to make it clear right now that I'm not interested in Jack Hunter the man, only in Jack Hunter the sportsman. If this is going to work, you'll have to follow my instructions to the letter and never question my methods."

There was nothing like laying your cards on the table, Jack thought. Tess might look like Diana, goddess of the hunt, but he suspected her teaching methods would more closely resemble those of a marble-hearted Marine instructor. He sensed an insecurity beneath her flinty facade and tried to lighten the moment. "I'm all yours for a month. Please feel free to do with me as you will."

"What I plan to do," she drawled, "is teach you enough wilderness skills to enable you to go on deluding your so-called fans for a little longer. That way you can continue to earn your ridiculously high salary long enough to pay me the exceedingly reasonable fee I'm charging you for said skills."

Jack admired her honesty, brutal as it was. "I'm not completely ignorant about hunting and fishing," he defended. "I've done a lot of studying on those subjects since I began writing for the show. I have the theories down pat, I just need some hands-on experience."

Trying not to think about what other connotations the term "hands-on experience" might entail, Tess glanced meaningfully at his injury. "Right."

"Are we nearly there? My leg's beginning to hurt like a son—"

"Almost." She fished around in her shirt pocket and dropped a metal slug in his lap.

"What's this?" he asked when he'd retrieved it.

"The bullet that passed through your flesh. I dug it out of the chair while you were in the bathroom. I thought you might like to bite it."

"Did you use your teeth or your fingernails?"

"My pocketknife."

"Figures. Just shut up and drive."

For once Tess did as directed. Considering the stress he was under, she would make allowances for his surly attitude. Pain might be the least of his problems once the hospital staff started firing their questions.

"Was it new?" she asked curiously as she turned into the hospital parking lot.

He glanced at her, puzzled. "Was what new?"

"The gun."

"New to me," he admitted.

"Great," she muttered, helping him out of the car. "You're not only a tenderfoot, you're a klutz."

"I am not a klutz, I merely made a—"

"I know, I know. A mistake." His arm circled her waist and Tess felt a silly heat where his body contacted hers. When she noticed that his hand seemed to accidently brush against areas of her anatomy that he had no business brushing against, she snapped at him. "What are you grinning about?"

He removed the offending hand and wiped the smile from his face in a hurry. "That wasn't a grin, it was a grimace of pain."

Unconvinced, she muttered, "It better be."

They entered the emergency room and the tired-looking nurse on duty gave Jack a stack of forms to complete. He did the best he could from his awkward position on a paper-covered gurney, then handed the clipboard to Tess. "Would you do the rest, please? By the way, is Tess short for something?"

"Since I've seen you in your underwear, please feel free to call me Tess." She read over some of the answers he had filled in on the questionnaire. "How can you live in Chicago and work in Colorado? Isn't that a long commute?"

"Keep your voice down," he whispered. "I gave my parents' address."

"Why?"

He looked at her as if there was no end to her obtuseness. "Why do you think?"

"Oh, yeah." She clicked her tongue. "Occupation, writer. Why didn't you tell the truth and say you were a sharpshooter."

"Be quiet, will you?" In an unnaturally pleasant voice he added, "Ahh, here's the nurse, darling."

Before Tess could respond to that familiarity, the nurse tugged the white curtains around the gurney and smiled apologetically at her. "I'm sorry, but you'll have to wait in the other room. I need to clean the wound and get our patient ready for Dr. Lambert."

Jack grabbed Tess's hand with both of his. "Can't she stay? I need her with me." He still wasn't sure he could trust her to keep his secret if he let her out of his sight.

Wondering if all city folks were as suspicious as Jack Hunter, Tess frowned at him. "I'll be right outside the door."

"I want you here," he stated adamantly.

"Now, Mr. McIver," the nurse soothed. "You're going to be just fine. But if you want your wife to stay, she may."

Mr. McIver? Wife? Tess gasped. She should have taken a closer look at those forms she'd handed the nurse. "But, he isn't—" She was about to tell the nurse that Jack Hunter was certainly not a McIver, but before she could reveal what a liar he was, he interrupted.

"Thanks a lot." He gave the nurse his most charming smile. "We appreciate it."

After the woman left, he said, "I thought you were going to blow my cover by telling her my real name."

Tess folded her arms across her chest. "Lying comes easy to you, doesn't it?"

It never had before, but it was amazing what desperation could do to a man. "I wasn't lying."

"Oh no?"

"I just hedged a bit. I used to live in Chicago, and I am a writer." At her skeptical look he added, "I worked for a Chicago newspaper for five years before I moved to Denver. And I still write occasional scripts for the program."

"What about telling that nurse your name was McIver and that we were married."

"I couldn't use my real name. What was I supposed to call myself?"

"How about Al Capone?" she suggested wryly.

"And I didn't tell her we were married. She assumed that."

"You didn't correct her," Tess pointed out. "And you wouldn't let me do it, either."

''That's not the same as lying.'' The way Jack saw it, it fell somewhere in the gray area.

She leveled a steely gaze at him. ''You're even more impossible than I thought you'd be. You're a self-centered phony. And you lie like a rug. I'm tempted to send you packing.''

He was tempted to explain the difference between lying and creating fiction, but decided such subtlety would be lost on a woman who carried a pocketknife. He settled instead on admiring the way she moved, which was graceful even when she was mad. ''You can't do that. We have a deal.''

''Deals can be canceled.'' She meant it as a threat, but even as she said it, Tess knew she wouldn't follow through on it. As much as she hated it, Big Bear Lodge needed Jack Hunter.

''Or renegotiated.'' Jack was used to getting his way, but he'd have to handle Tess carefully. He didn't have time to look for another mentor. If he was going to survive the next thirty days and learn enough to become the sportsman he already claimed to be, he'd have to keep his mind on business—and off this maddeningly attractive woman.

They couldn't continue the discussion as the nurse returned and began cleaning Jack's wound. After that, the pain required his full attention.

Tess was worried. Considering how hard it was to stay mad at Jack, she would have to be careful around him. He was as appealing as he was irritating, and she didn't care one bit for such ambivalent feelings. She managed to act nonchalant as she watched the nurse at work. She stepped aside when the doctor came into the room, and winced sympathetically when a grimace creased Jack's handsome features.

"I think I'll get something cool to drink," she said suddenly.

"You aren't leaving." Jack's statement was more command than question, and Tess didn't take commands well.

"Only for a minute. I'll be right back," she muttered.

He watched her go. The attraction he felt managed to penetrate his pain and dance its way along his libido. She was unlike any woman he'd ever met, and he found her both intriguing and aggravating. Even if she didn't hold him in high regard, he instinctively felt he could trust her to keep this little debacle to herself. He certainly hoped so.

Tess leaned wearily against the soft drink machine and took a long swallow of root beer. As soon as the cool liquid slid down her throat she felt better, chiding herself for feeling squeamish because Jack was in pain. After all, she barely knew the man.

When a birdlike older lady walked up to the machine, Tess pushed herself out of the way with a muttered apology.

The lady adjusted the black wig she wore as if it were an ill-fitting hat. When she was satisfied with the results, she said, "Oh, I don't want a soda, dear. I'm just concerned about you. You looked upset, and I wondered if you might need someone to talk to."

Tess wasn't sure what to make of this stranger's concern, but smiled at the woman anyway. "Thanks, but I'm fine."

"I'm Madelyn Flame." The lady peered at Tess over gold-rimmed bifocals. "Everybody calls me Maddie."

Tess shook the tiny blue-veined hand and noted the woman's lively blue eyes. "Tess McIver."

"Nice to meet you, Tess."

"Are you waiting for someone?" The woman seemed determined to strike up a conversation, so Tess obliged, happy to have a reason not to think about Jack.

"Oh, no. I drive over here once a week or so and bring the staff cookies or brownies. I so enjoy gossiping with the nurses—if they're not too busy, that is. What are you in for, Tess?"

"Oh, it isn't me. My..." Even though the woman was just a lonely stranger, Tess couldn't forget her promise to Jack. As much as it pained her, she continued the story he had started. "My, er, husband had an accident."

"Your husband?" Maddie's eyes narrowed, but she smiled. "You say that as if you haven't been married long." Her prodding was gentle, but insistent.

"Not long at all." A flush of embarrassment crept over Tess's face.

Maddie grinned triumphantly. "You're newlyweds!"

"Very," Tess said dryly, thinking she had no idea just how *new*. "The ink is barely dry on the forms."

"Do you live here in Vail or are you on your honeymoon?"

Tess, who believed in scrupulous honesty, grew more irritated at Jack by the moment. She'd only known him a few hours and already his influence had her inventing half-truths with ease. But she couldn't lie about anything so intimate; she couldn't even think about it. "We didn't take a honeymoon."

"Oh, I see. So you live here. What do you do?" Maddie was definitely persistent.

"We run Big Bear Lodge about forty miles from here." Tess meant her and Bitterroot, but she knew Maddie would assume she meant her and her husband.

"I've heard of your place. A hunting lodge, isn't it?"

"Yes."

"You know," Maddie said conspiratorially. "I'm a nature lover myself. I often go on nature hikes. Maybe I could drop in on you sometime and tromp around your woods."

"Sure," Tess agreed, thinking the woman must be lonely indeed if she was willing to invite herself for a visit. But surely she wouldn't drive that far to renew such a fleeting acquaintance.

"I hope it's nothing serious. With your husband, I mean."

Tess didn't want to discuss Hunter. "Not really. But I'd better get back. He's probably wondering where I am." She gave Maddie a friendly wave and left her standing by the soft drink machine. When she glanced back, she noticed the woman was busily scribbling something in a notebook. No doubt she was penning a visit to Big Bear Lodge onto her appointment calendar.

Tess returned just as the doctor finished up, and he gave her a list of instructions and told her what danger signs to watch for. He followed the nurse out of the room, leaving Tess to help her *husband* get dressed.

Jack gave her his wallet and sent her to the business office to pay the bill while a police officer summoned by the admitting nurse questioned him for the necessary report. A few more evasions, a couple of half-truths and a lot of embarrassment later, they were free to leave. Given a shot for pain, Jack slept all the way back to the lodge.

Tess stopped to give a progress report to Bitterroot. She took full advantage of the opportunity to tell her father that his charge was turning out to be more nuisance than he was worth. She gathered up a few things she might need and kissed the old man good-night before driving Jack to his cabin.

She'd briefly considered putting him up at the main lodge, but had quickly dismissed the idea. There were only three bedrooms, and one of those had a leaky hole in the roof since Bitterroot's accident. She couldn't ask her father, who was ill-tempered as it was at being incapacitated, to give up his room. And she wouldn't consider having him in her own bed, even if she wasn't in it.

The best thing was to try and make him comfortable in his own cabin. She glanced at Jack drowsing uneasily in the seat beside her. Recalling the doctor's instructions, she knew she would have to spend the night by his side. There were no phones in the rough cabins, and if he awoke in trouble in the middle of the night, someone had to be there to help him.

Who was she kidding? Even sleeping he was an unconscionably handsome and vital man. The only person likely to get into trouble here tonight was her.

And that trouble was spelled H-u-n-t-e-r.

Chapter Three

"We're here." Tess roused Jack from his drug-induced slumber with all the fanfare she could muster. The doctor had given him an injection for pain and a packet of pills to see him through the next twenty-four hours. Incapacitated as he was, she had the devil's own time getting him out of the car and into the cabin.

Relieved to finally put some physical distance between them, she pried his arm from around her shoulders. "Now that you're safely home, can you get into bed on your own?"

Jack bit back the retort that this rustic place could never be his home, and concentrated on the pain that was returning with a vengeance now that he was fully awake. He hobbled over to the half-size bed and plopped down. "The way this leg feels, I'll never walk again."

"Oh," she scoffed. "I wouldn't say that. The worst is probably yet to come."

"Thanks for the reassurance. You have the gracious bedside manner of a real doctor. Dr. Frankenstein." Painfully he turned on his side, putting his back to her.

Tess grinned. Judging by the caustic comments, he was in full possession of his wits, and she could put off checking his pupils for signs of dilation until he was in a more cooperative mood. According to the doctor, delayed shock was possible during the first twenty-four hours following a traumatic injury. At this point, internal hemorrhaging was unlikely, but she was supposed to check regularly, just in case. It was going to be a long night, and she had the sneaking suspicion that Jack Hunter wouldn't be a good patient.

She sat down in the bushwhacked chair and thought about her options. She should go to the lodge, phone his producer and demand that the studio send a real nurse to take over the burden of his care. But Tess made no move to do so. She'd given her word.

The shooting was accidental and his wound would heal quickly. The main concern now was infection, and she was determined not to risk even one small portion of his splendid anatomy to such a fate.

Irritation at her predicament mounted with each passing moment. Despite the protectiveness she felt toward him, she was not attracted to Jack Hunter!

Jack had hoped that sleep would overcome him, but the throbbing in his leg was intense. He kept his attention riveted on the uncurtained window near his bed. It was completely dark out there, and the crisp, rarefied air was filled with insect sounds as the creatures showed up for the night shift.

Being a city dweller, he couldn't name them and felt no compulsion to do so. He was out of his element, and he missed the blare of horns and the screech of tires. Suddenly nostalgic for jet engines and train whistles, he wondered how he'd ever survive so much tranquility. That and the proximity of Tess McIver might very well do him in.

Jack turned over, forgetting for a moment that he was wounded.

Tess stood up when she heard him groan.

"Where are you going?" he asked, still unwilling to trust her completely.

"To the sink in the corner. I thought you might need a glass of water to wash down a pain pill."

"You're not planning to break your promise by going to the lodge and making a phone call after I fall asleep, are you?"

She clamped down on her temper with effort. Only a dishonest person could be so distrustful. "No, I don't break promises. I'll admit I thought about it, but I gave you my word."

"Thanks." He had the good grace to duck his head sheepishly. "I'm sorry."

"Apology accepted." Tess made sure the bandage was secure, then fussed with his covers and plumped up his pillows. He was such a grouch. She wondered if he was that way all the time, or if it was just her. Maybe he wished he had someone more sympathetic taking care of him.

Jack felt genuinely chastened. Tess had already had ample opportunity to blow the whistle on him, but hadn't. Therefore he had no reason to doubt her, and he couldn't understand why he was behaving so abominably. "I know it's hard to believe, but I'm not usually so paranoid. I really am grateful for all you've done."

"You're welcome," she said, realizing that half an apology was better than none. "Is there anything else you need?"

Jack grinned and his eyes twinkled mischievously. Her stomach fluttered against her will when he said, "Ask me that question again when I feel a little stronger."

The man was amazing. Surely he wasn't thinking what she thought he was. "How about a bowl of soup?"

"Good idea." Soup had been the last thing on his mind as Tess had fussed over him, and his feelings confused him. She just wasn't his type. He usually went for softer, more pliable women, so why was he so damned attracted to this female Grizzly Adams?

He knew the answer. It was because he liked her spirit and admired her strength. He sensed something special in Tess McIver, a rare combination of toughness and vulnerability. But most of all, he was drawn to her integrity—something totally new for Jack. In the past he'd been attracted to women because of their faces or their legs or their extraordinary chest measurements—all the external, superficial stuff.

But after only a few hours with Tess, he was seeing internal qualities. Not that there was anything wrong with her outside. The problem was, she sent so many mixed signals it was hard to get a fix on her.

Like a moment ago. Before she had averted her gaze, he'd seen something sad in her eyes. That look of fragility made him feel especially tender toward her, and he was pretty sure she didn't normally inspire tenderness in men.

Maybe it was an illusion or a weird side effect of the pain pills, because when he'd looked again, all he had seen was fierce determination and flashing pride before she turned her back and began preparing his food.

He shrugged out of his shirt and took care not to jostle his leg as he maneuvered between the covers and removed his jeans. It was warm in the little cabin, but he pulled the sheet over his lap for modesty's sake. He kept his gaze on Tess the whole time, noting the way her backside swayed as she vigorously stirred the soup. He couldn't help wondering if there was a man in her life.

Before he could stop himself he blurted, "Are you involved with anyone?"

"No. Single men are pretty scarce around here." She kept her back to him, not wanting him to see how pleased she was that he'd broached the subject first. Now maybe she could ask him the same question.

He was disappointed when she wasn't forthcoming with a few more pertinent facts. But since she wasn't his type, he'd just mind his own business.

She strove for indifference when she asked, "Do you have a wife who should be notified about your accident?"

"Not anymore." His tone implied that he liked it that way. "And if we were still married, she'd be the last person I'd tell. She's more efficient at spreading news than a wire service."

She balanced a tray across his lap and settled in the bedside chair. With all his flirtatious innuendos, she should have guessed that he was just another divorced man on the prowl for new conquests.

"I really can't see why you're making such a big deal about keeping this a secret. These things happen," she told him. "Why, last year alone there were over seventeen hundred injuries caused by hunting accidents."

"Maybe among amateurs, but I'm supposed to be an expert."

"Like they say, to err is human."

"Certain things might come out that I wouldn't want divulged." His grin was ornery. "Like, I wasn't even hunting at the time. How many 'sitting' accidents occur in any given year?"

Jack studied the casual expression on her face, then with extra emphasis he added, "Don't you see? I could've been ruined. Professionally."

She felt drawn into the intensity of his dark gaze, but what bothered her most was the fact that she was enjoying it. She quipped, "You were damn near ruined anyway. Physically."

He groaned. Suddenly he wasn't hungry anymore—for anything. Careful not to disturb his leg, he set the tray aside. "Don't remind me."

"How did it happen?" She might as well find out now just how much work she had ahead of her. "Really."

"I was getting to know my weapon like all the books say to do. I was learning the feel of it, getting used to the weight of it in my hands. I loaded it, unloaded it and reloaded it several times this afternoon. Just as the reference books directed." Jack picked up a hefty tome from his bedside table and tapped the title for emphasis.

Tess groaned. "The first rule of hunting safety is never point the muzzle at anything you don't intend to shoot. Don't you know that?"

"Of course I *know* that, I just didn't *do* that. I wasn't planning to fire."

"I've seen you skeet shooting on your Sunday afternoon show." She wouldn't admit that she'd been almost spellbound watching him on-screen. His role on the program was not a glamorous one, but the camera loved him just the same. Even outdoors in uncertain light it had shown him to advantage.

Oblivious to human imperfections, it lingered over the rugged planes of his face. It picked up the spark of humor in his eyes and captured every virile movement. It made the most of the reassuring confidence he exuded. The confidence that was all a sham.

"It wasn't me. Well," he qualified, "it was me on-screen, but I didn't do the actual shooting. When I held and aimed the rifles, they weren't loaded."

She opened her mouth, and he held up his hand to stop the words he knew were coming. "I know, I know. A person should always treat a firearm as if it is loaded, even when it isn't. And you can be damn sure I won't forget that in the future."

"I hope not."

"The problem is I never actually do any of the real shooting. The studio won't allow it because of my lack of experience. An excellent marksman, a gifted camera crew and a very clever film editor are responsible for making me look good."

"I see."

"I don't think you do."

"I'm sorry but it's just disappointing to find out it's all faked."

"Not faked. It's an illusion. That's what television is about. You wouldn't feel disappointed if you learned your favorite actor didn't really dodge bullets or duke it out with bad guys, would you?"

"Of course not. That's different."

"It's not so different when you think about it."

"So why are you here? Why change an illusion?"

Jack grinned crookedly. "I guess I want to be a hero."

She glanced pointedly at his leg. "And dodge bullets?"

"I just don't like to disappoint people. Especially beautiful women."

There he goes again, Tess thought. The man has a real knack for turning innocent conversation into something more. "That's good to know—from a teacher's standpoint, I mean. So, you're a novice with firearms. Do you have any experience with wildlife?"

He frowned. Things had always come easy for him, no matter what he wanted he usually got it. All his life no one had expected more from him than he was willing to deliver, but Tess McIver would. And she would make him expect it, too.

He did what he always did when he was uneasy, he turned flippant. "I once helped hunt for my nephew's sociopathic hamster in a high-rise condominium. Does that count?"

Tess shook her head. "How about fish? What's your favorite?"

"Trout—broiled with butter and served with lemon on the side."

"You don't know a fishing pole from a tent pole," she guessed.

"Wrong. I've seen lots of fishing poles and even held a few in my very own hands on camera."

"But you didn't actually fish," she surmised.

"Endorsements for tackle manufacturers."

"This is amazing. How did you manage to end up hosting a wildlife show?"

"It's a long story."

"Since I'm stuck here all night anyway, I have nothing but time," she said ungraciously.

"I suppose I owe you that much." Jack shrugged, resigned to his fate. "When I came out to Colorado from Chicago, I got a job as a scriptwriter for a show called *Walker's Wildlife* on KRVO-TV—"

"Wait a minute," she interrupted. "Let me get a cup of coffee. Want one?"

Jack nodded assent and continued his story. "During contract negotiations the star, Kent Walker, demanded on outrageous pay raise. When the producers refused, he quit."

"Bitterroot mentioned as much. He got the full scoop from the tabloids. He even subscribes to the *Stargazer's Gazette*. I was surprised when a local story got into a national publication."

"They have to fill pages somehow and any star, no matter how dim its radiance, is fair game," Jack said cynically. "After Kent left, there was total chaos at the station, and everyone was given the rest of the day off. As I was leaving, one of the producers cornered me and started talking about how I'd be perfect for the job. I declined, explaining I was a writer and not a performer, and that I wasn't personally acquainted with the wilderness or its many creatures."

"What did she say to that?"

Jack looked up in surprise. "How did you know it was a woman?"

"Just a wild hunch," she said innocently. Jack Hunter was the kind of man a woman would be compelled to approach if she were in trouble. "Go on."

"I told her I'd rather work behind the camera than in front of it. But she said she wanted me. I explained that in the course of writing for the show I'd learned a lot about guns, hunting, fishing and other macho stuff but it was all theory."

"You had knowledge but not experience."

"Exactly. That's what I told Marcia Murphy. But she insisted it didn't matter. She said they had a staff who could take care of it. According to her, I *looked* creditable and the audience would love me. All I had to do was memorize my lines and emote sinewy confidence. Whatever that is."

"You do look the part," she admitted grudgingly. He probably got tons of fan letters from women who couldn't care less about the outdoors. The first time she'd seen him on the screen, she hadn't realized what the program was about until after the third commercial for insect repellent.

"I tried to talk Marcia out of it, but she insisted. A little thing like my not knowing how to handle a gun couldn't change her mind. But I held out. It just didn't feel right."

"Then . . ." she prompted.

"Then she sweetened the negotiations with a lucrative salary."

"Ahh, money—the great seducer."

"Don't be so judgmental. I needed it to bail myself out of the postdivorce financial pits. But I didn't accept until Norton asked me to do it. The show was his brainchild, and if they couldn't replace Walker it would be canceled."

"Who's Norton?"

"Norton Greene is the head writer on the show. He's also an old friend. We grew up together back in Chicago. Now *there's* a real sportsman."

"If he's knowledgeable enough to write the show, why doesn't he host it?"

"They turned him down. Marcia said he looked too much like an accountant. So when he asked me to do it as a favor to him, I couldn't refuse. When Clarice and I split up, Norton got me the scriptwriting job that allowed me to leave my troubles, namely Clarice, in Chicago. Besides, I really didn't expect the show to last

this long with me hosting, let alone become syndi-
cated.''

"Why didn't Norton teach you what you need to
know?''

"We go back twenty years, and I didn't want to
jeopardize our friendship,'' he said with a laugh.
"Also, I was afraid he'd go easy on me. Which is
something I don't have to worry about you doing.''

She grinned. "I know what you said about being a
hero, but why go to so much trouble? Male ego
again?''

"It's the principle of the thing. I would rather have
had the lessons before I did the first episode but there
wasn't time. And lately, I feel like I've been cheating
the show's fans. So here I am.''

The man was worried about principles? Maybe he
had scruples after all. "You could leave the show.''

"I promised Norton, and I'm not a quitter. I'm determined to learn if it kills me...'' Jack's what-am-I-
saying gaze collided with Tess's you've-got-to-be-
kidding look and they laughed companionably.

"Enough about me. Tell me what a nice girl like you
is doing way out here all alone.''

"I was born here. I've lived here all my life and I
have no desire to live anywhere else. I'm not alone, I
have my father. I don't have a man because I choose
not to. End of story.'' Tess fidgeted. "You know, I've
learned a lot about you, but you never have told me
what happened after that clip jammed.''

Evidently that was all he was going to hear about
Tess. "You have a one-track mind, woman,'' he

teased. "Don't get me wrong. That can be a real bonus once it gets on the right track."

"The story," she prompted.

"You want gory details." At her nod, he continued. "The books and Norton said that in time the gun would become an extension of my body." He stopped when he saw the look in her eyes. "What are you smirking about?"

"Nothing." It seemed ironic that he might have lost a very important part of that body had he been any less talented a marksman. She glanced at the pistol on the table. "Do you plan to hunt with handguns on your show?"

"Of course not. I thought I'd start with something small and less intimidating. Anyway, the clip jammed. It wouldn't go in and it wouldn't come out. I pounded it with the heel of my hand. It finally gave way, but the gun discharged a bullet at the same time. The rest you know."

"But *how* were you holding it?" she persisted, unsure why she was goading him so.

"In my lap," he groaned. In retrospect it had been a stupid thing to do. The fact that he knew it only added to his chagrin.

She began to laugh. Because he was so embarrassed, she tried to stifle her mirth, but it was no use. "I'm sorry," she offered. "But—"

"No, please don't say it," he begged with a grin. "I feel foolish enough as it is."

"I really am sorry," she said with an escaped giggle. They'd talked for quite a while; it was late and Jack looked tired. It was proof of his stamina that he'd been bantering as long as he had. She stood and took the tray to the sink. "Try to rest."

"I think I will." He felt drained as well as humiliated. He leaned his head against the pillows. Now that he didn't have the distraction of conversation, the pain was too intense to ignore.

Tess retrieved a flashlight from the bedside table. "I need to check for pupil dilation." She examined each eye, trying not to notice how brown and burning they really were.

"Why?" he asked. "I don't have a concussion."

"We can't rule out shock yet. Besides, you were released in my care and I have instructions. How's the pain?" A couple of hours had passed since he'd last taken medication.

"Pretty bad," he admitted.

"You can take another pill."

"I'll wait." Jack didn't like taking any kind of drugs, and he wasn't so sure he wanted to sleep after all. What he'd really like to do was talk to Tess McIver. He wanted to know everything there was to know about her. He surprised himself—he'd never been that interested in a woman's history before. "Don't you ever get lonely out here?"

"No. Bitterroot is good company, and most of the time the lodge is full of clients."

"That's not what I meant. Don't you ever—"

"Hardly ever," Tess quickly interrupted. "I think I'm tired of this conversation. Besides, you need your rest."

"Are you really going to stay here tonight?"

"Doctor's orders. If you need anything, I'll be right over there in that chair."

Jack closed his eyes wearily. "Okay, but if you hear moaning and groaning, don't be alarmed. It'll just be my impersonation of a man in the throes of agony."

"I knew it. You are in pain, aren't you?"

"Yeah." His leg began to throb with renewed intensity. "I think I will have another painkiller after all."

"Which kind?" she asked innocently. "The one the doctor prescribed or the bottle with your picture on the label?" Without waiting for an answer, she handed him a glass of water and a tablet. She shouldn't tease him; it wasn't fair. Jack Hunter was turning out to be a pretty nice guy; a little too nice for her peace of mind.

When he reached for the water his hand touched hers, and she quickly pulled it back.

"I make you uncomfortable, don't I?" he asked.

Add perceptiveness to his list of qualities. "Not at all." She bustled about, straightening his covers and plumping his pillows again.

"I think you're as attracted to me as I am to you. The sad thing is that neither of us is happy about it."

"That's crazy."

"What, the idea of being attracted to me or being unhappy about it?"

Tess rolled her eyes. "Take your medicine."

He swallowed the pill, but kept his gaze trained on her as he downed the water. When he finished he pushed the glass into her outstretched hand. He wanted to pursue this interesting line of conversation, but he sensed she might abandon him to his fate if he did.

She turned out the bedside lamp and retreated to her corner across the small room. She sank tiredly onto the chair, vastly relieved at having even a small physical distance between them. Hunter was not an easy man to resist up close.

She glanced at the bed and the silent man. At least he was resting quietly. She'd have to repeat the eye test in two hours, but she hoped he would sleep until then.

"Tess?" he asked drowsily sometime later.

She hurried to the bed and bent over him. "Yes, what's wrong?"

"I just wanted to see if you were still here," he said in a sleep-husky tone.

"I'm not going anywhere," she whispered. She brushed a lock of hair from his forehead and noticed that his skin was slightly warm. The doctor had warned her about the onset of fever and its effects. She stood for a moment, gazing at him. He looked so defenseless lying there that she scooted the big chair to the side of the bed. He might wake up again and she didn't want him to think he was alone.

Jack rolled his head on the pillow. "Is that where you're sleeping?" he asked groggily.

"I wouldn't call it that. More like resting till it's time to wake you again. Sleep while you can."

"How can I, knowing how uncomfortable you are in that damn chair? There's room for you on the bed." Jack raised weakly onto one elbow. "I promise not to take advantage of the situation. I doubt if I could in my condition, no matter how badly I might want to."

"I'm not worried about that. If I were to lie down I'd really fall asleep, and I might not wake up in time to check you. Now go to sleep."

He laid back on his pillow and after a few minutes the steady rise and fall of his chest told her that he had.

Moonbeams silvered through the windows, filling the small cabin with a mystical light. Outside, crickets chirped and the wind rustled in the pine boughs. The distant shriek of a night-hunting bird splintered the silence, but Jack did not stir. He was sleeping soundly. Satisfied, Tess leaned back in the overstuffed chair and dozed.

An inner alarm woke her a couple of hours later. Once again she leaned over Jack with the flashlight. "Jack?"

He moaned slightly.

"Jack," she insisted. "I need to check your eyes again."

"Okay." He tried to cooperate but failed.

"Come on," she coaxed. "Open your eyes for a moment, then you can go back to sleep."

"I can't." His words were slurred.

She put her hand on his shoulder and shook him gently. "Jack, open those big brown eyes."

Flushed and aching, he wanted only to sleep. Somehow his life depended on it. "Later."

"Do you want me to take you back to the hospital?" she threatened.

Further speech seemed too difficult, but with considerable effort he opened his weighty lids.

She performed her ritual with the flashlight. "Now you can go back to sleep. You have two more hours before I have to torture you again." She smiled and couldn't resist pushing the persistent lock of hair off his forehead. He was warmer than before, but still not alarmingly feverish. She slumped back in the lumpy chair.

Sometime later, Tess jerked awake. Pale predawn light suffused the room with its glow, and she checked her watch guiltily. She'd slept for over five hours. She shook Jack's shoulder and reached for the flashlight.

He groaned.

"Jack?"

"Not again," he moaned.

"Yes, again," she insisted. "I'm sorry, but it has to be done."

He mumbled something unintelligible.

"Come on, Jack," she cajoled. "Open up and let me see what's going on in there."

His lids fluttered open. She was satisfied with the size of his pupils, but alarmed that he was shivering. "How do you feel?"

Like not talking was how he felt. Then Tess's cool hands touched his face and she was asking him questions. He tried to concentrate so he could answer, but words were too difficult.

"Jack! You're burning up." She cursed herself for neglecting to bring a thermometer to the cabin.

Her voice penetrated his foggy brain and he could tell she was upset. "I don't have a fever," he said, his teeth chattering. "I'm freezing."

"Damn!" Tess muttered as she removed the blankets from the bed, leaving him covered by a thin sheet.

"Hey!" he protested. "I'm freezing, I said."

After she made him swallow a couple of aspirin tablets, she sat on the side of the bed and wrapped her arms around him. "We've got to break the fever," she said. "Believe me."

Jack struggled weakly out of her grasp to pull up the sheet, but she held him back, and eventually, he burrowed into her for the warmth and comfort she provided.

Long after his shivers subsided and he slept, Tess stayed where she was, holding him in her arms. She allowed her lips to caress his forehead until she was satisfied that his temperature had returned to normal.

Finally, relieved and physically drained, Tess slept with the man. A man she barely knew.

Chapter Four

Warm sunshine streamed through the window and beamed down on Jack's shoulder, but it was the even warmer body pressed against him that brought him to full wakefulness. A quick glance around the rough cabin oriented him to his location, but it did not explain the woman snuggled at his side.

Her weight impaired the circulation in his arm, but he lay still, knowing that if he moved it Tess would wake up. Much of last night was lost to the medication he'd taken, and he had no idea why she was in his bed. But instinct told him she would not be happy with the situation. She sighed in her sleep, and her limp hand nestled familiarly in the hair on his chest. Jack held his breath until she settled more comfortably beside him.

He didn't know what time it was, but the sun was bright and the birds were making a racket outside.

He'd figured Tess for an early riser, and the fact that she was dead to the world meant she'd spent a sleepless night caring for him. The thought moved him to unheard-of tenderness, and he watched her sleep for several moments before gently sweeping splayed auburn curls away from her face with his free hand.

In order to see her better, he angled his body more fully toward hers. Her eyebrows were dark and well-defined, rising to a peak over the bluest eyes he'd ever seen. Funny how he remembered their vivid hue even when they were closed.

Luxurious lashes, too long and thick to be real, fanned over high rosy cheekbones. But they had to be real; Tess McIver was not the kind of woman to practice artifice. Her lips were full, slightly parted and softly pink. He couldn't tear his gaze away from them and wondered what she'd do if he kissed her.

The arm on which she lay so trustingly tightened of its own volition, drawing her closer. Before he quite realized it, her lips were only a breath away from his. He touched them with his fingertip, then stroked her cheek with the back of his fingers. Her skin was warm and smooth, tempting in its softness.

He couldn't remember ever wanting a woman more. But this was a different kind of wanting. He wanted to know everything about her. To be privy to her thoughts, her feelings, her hopes and dreams. He wanted her touch. The ache he felt had nothing to do with his bullet wound, and desire battled principle for a reluctant moment before he drew his hand away and settled it companionably on her shoulder.

Tess awoke the moment Jack's hand drifted through her hair, but she pretended to sleep so she could figure out how best to handle the situation. She'd never awakened in bed with a man before, much less a strange one, and she wasn't quite sure what to do. Should she yawn and stretch and offer to make coffee as if nothing out of the ordinary had happened?

Maybe she should resume the role of nurse and explain matter-of-factly that she'd climbed into bed with him to comfort him through his fever chills. Evidently her tactics had worked; the hand that had caressed her face was deliciously warm but not unduly hot.

But such unorthodox nursing methods would not explain why she had sprawled all over him in the night, her body clinging to his like plastic wrap. And more appalling, they would not explain why she was so loathe to slip out of his embrace. All she had to do was roll over and ease out of bed. Which was what she intended to do. Soon.

Despite the numbness in his arm, Jack didn't feel too bad. The throbbing in his leg had become a dull ache, and he felt clearheaded and alert for the first time since the accident. He knew he should wake her up and put an end to this torture, but he enjoyed holding Tess and wasn't ready to relinquish her just yet.

Even though she was fully dressed, he felt the heat of her body. One of her long, slender legs was thrown over his, and her right hand lay on his chest. Her tall body matched his perfectly, as if they belonged together. As inexplicable as it was, they were bound by a magic thread neither of them understood. Jack's heart raced at the implications of such thoughts.

Pressed as she was against his chest, Tess couldn't help but notice the acceleration of Jack's heart rate. There was no telling what he was thinking, and the longer she stayed in his arms, the riskier things would get. No doubt he had misinterpreted her actions and probably thought she wanted him. She couldn't allow that, she'd have to get up. Now.

Hoping she hadn't lingered too long, she peeled herself away from him with a great deal more determination than should have been necessary. Embarrassed beyond words, she blinked up into warm brown eyes. Faults he might have, but there was nothing wrong with Jack Hunter's eyes.

"Good morning." The eyes in question crinkled at the corners, and she decided there should be a law against men whose good-natured grins only enhanced their looks.

"G'morning," she mumbled.

He leaned onto one elbow and gazed down at her. "Your bedside manner has undergone a dramatic improvement in the night."

"I can explain all this." Tess scrambled out of bed as if she had found something unpleasant crawling on the sheets. "You had a fever and chills. I was trying to help you break it."

"You succeeded." Jack chuckled at her nervous display, knowing that this was a side Tess rarely revealed.

"I didn't hurt you, did I?" she worried.

"Not yet," Jack answered softly, fully aware that there was a chance she would break his heart.

"I'll make coffee," she offered, eager to change the subject.

Jack watched her closely as she banged cupboard doors looking for the coffee tin. She seemed extremely wide awake for someone who'd been soundly asleep only a few seconds ago. "Thanks. I don't feel human until I've had at least two cups," he baited.

"I know what you mean. It takes me forever to become alert when I wake up." Too late she realized she might as well have blurted out the fact that she'd been aware of all the snuggling. No doubt he assumed she had faked sleep because she enjoyed being in his arms. She turned her back so he wouldn't notice the embarrassed flush creeping over her face.

Jack accepted the steaming mug she thrust at him. She seemed to want to keep her distance now and disappeared into the bathroom without a word. When she returned a few minutes later, there wasn't a trace of pink left in her cheeks.

Thinking they'd been through enough together not to worry about modesty, Jack eased out of bed, grabbed a clean pair of jeans from the closet and hobbled into the bathroom. The short trip required every scrap of willpower he could muster. He'd felt pretty good lying in bed, but that had all changed once he'd attained a vertical posture. He'd thought he was healing quickly, that he would be okay. But by the time he'd dressed, washed his face and brushed his teeth, he knew he wouldn't make it. He would die. Right here in this boondock bathroom.

He flung open the door and managed another pain-filled step, sweat beading on his forehead and upper lip. The room started to dim, and he waited for the nausea to pass, hoping he wouldn't embarrass himself by keeling over. To someone who had always taken his physical strength for granted, the weakness was more annoying than the pain.

Tess saw Jack's pallor and rushed to his side. As she supported him, she warned, "Don't you dare pass out on me, Hunter. I'm not sure I can manage you by myself." She helped him stumble to the bed, then went into the bathroom for a cool wet cloth to bathe his face. "Feel better?"

"A little," he muttered.

"You don't have a fever." She pressed her fingers to his wrist and felt the steady pulse. "It's the pain, isn't it?"

"I hate to complain, but it does hurt," he said in understatement. "I think those pills made me woozy. I'll just try some aspirin this time."

She found them for him and he gladly accepted the tablets and some water. "Maybe you should stay in bed today and give your system a chance to recuperate."

"What? No thirty-mile hikes?" he teased.

"You should be recovered enough to start work on Monday. We'll stay right on schedule. In the meantime, I can give you basic background information while you're resting."

"You don't cut a man much slack," he said peevishly. "But I guess a bullet wound wouldn't slow down someone of pioneer stock."

Tess was still embarrassed about sleeping with him and about pretending to be asleep. She was also angry that he'd had the good grace not to make a big deal out of it. She hadn't expected consideration or sensitivity from him. But maybe to him it was no big deal.

"You'll be all right if you stay prone until you get your legs back," she told him. "I need to go to the lodge and see about Pop. He can't get around too well himself."

He raised a brow speculatively. "I know why you're in such a hurry to get out of here."

"Do you?" she snapped.

"You're afraid I'll make a pass, right?"

Tess shook her head too vehemently. "No, I'm not."

Innocence filled his eyes. "Oh. Then you're worried you might make one?"

"No. I have work to do. You hired me to teach you wilderness skills, not to be your personal attendant."

"You're right," he said contritely. "But would you mind if I did?"

"Did what?"

"Make a pass at you?"

"Yes. And I'm getting tired of you talking about it all the time. Get it over with, for Pete's sake, so I can push you away and tell you there can be nothing between us but business. It'll save time all around."

"I don't believe you. I detect a whole different message when I touch you."

"Then your antenna is faulty. Probably worn-out from overuse."

"You've decided not to give in to your impulses too soon, right?"

"You're the one with ESP. You tell me." She glared at him indignantly.

"You want to be absolutely sure that I understand you're not 'that kind of girl.' "

"You have a lot of gall." She made to turn away, but he caught her wrist easily in his hand and pulled her down with a plop on the bed. She sat there, unwilling to make a scene by struggling with him.

"I'm perceptive." Jack had decided that since she could resist charm he'd have to be honest as well. "Given the chemistry between us, I wouldn't be opposed to a little hanky-panky under the pines."

"Of all the nerve!" Tess spluttered.

"I'm willing to suffer through whatever abbreviated courtship you deem necessary." He rubbed his index finger gently under her chin.

She threw off his hand and stood abruptly, fully intending to slam out the cabin door. After three paces in that direction, she turned and faced him. "You know, for a while there I thought I'd misjudged you. But I was wrong. You are every bit as self-absorbed, conceited and arrogant as I first assumed."

Jack was more amused than offended. "Are you finished?"

"Almost." Tess was more exasperated than angry. "For your information, I would rather walk barefoot over smoldering pinecones than engage in hanky-panky with you."

Jack burst out laughing, and the sudden action caused a twitch of pain. "Ouch!"

"Serves you right," she said dismissively. "Get those thoughts out of your mind. While you're here you'll need all your strength just to match the pace I set for you."

He regarded her with interest. Obviously, soft and tender was out and tough and relentless was back in. He found the verbal sparring stimulating. Now he knew what he'd been missing with all those acquiescent females he'd dated. "Survival is serious business, huh?"

"Very serious," she confirmed on her way to the door.

"Tess?" he asked when it was clear that she really meant to leave. "Does this mean I won't get any?"

"What?" she yelped as she spun around.

"Breakfast," he said with a wounded expression. "Don't I get any breakfast?"

Tess was not accustomed to matching wits with a man, and she was getting weary of the game. "Oh, forgive me. Of course you get breakfast. It's all part of the deluxe accommodation package." She stalked to the cupboard, flung it open, and rummaged through the food supplies he'd brought along.

"Here you go, ace. *Bon appétit.*" With that she tossed a cellophane-wrapped twig into his lap.

"Thanks." He didn't sound too grateful as he eyed the mummified piece of beef jerky.

"You're welcome. And don't get used to room service. You're on your own for a while. I'll stop by this afternoon and we'll do whatever can be done while you're in bed."

''Promise?'' Jack knew better than to comment on that loaded remark, but he couldn't resist. She made it too simple.

''You're impossible.''

''Actually I'm pretty easy. But you have to be nice.''

''Oh, for Pete's sake. Just rest. Or take a cold shower.'' Tess felt only slight remorse at leaving Jack alone. Anyone who was well enough to think about hanky-panky was well enough to fend for himself for a few hours.

He grinned when the door slammed on its rusty hinges. The pain he'd felt earlier had subsided as soon as he'd taken his weight off his leg, and he was feeling almost frisky again. She was probably right. By Monday he should be recovered enough to work. But that was forty-eight hours away, and Jack wasn't used to being alone.

When Tess returned to the cabin later that afternoon she found Jack fully dressed and reclining on his bed, reading a gun safety manual. She refrained from pointing out that it was about time. He had shaved, and his face bore no signs of its earlier pallor. In fact he looked better than she had yet seen him look.

That was only part of the problem. The hardest thing was ignoring his teasing remarks and taking care of business. But asking Hunter to be serious, she soon learned, was like asking the mountain sky to change colors. It could happen, but it wasn't something a mere mortal could control.

After an hour Tess's nerves were as taut as mandolin strings, and Jack insisted on strumming them at every opportunity. She tried again to gain his interest.

"Did you know that game hunters pay over $281.9 million a year for conservation? Hunters do more to aid wildlife than any other group in America."

Norton had already told him that, but Jack played ignorant. He enjoyed the company. "How is that?"

"The money paid for hunting licenses supports state game departments, which are responsible for the major conservation programs in the country. And the money for each Federal Duck Stamp purchased is used by the government to buy and lease wetlands for waterfowl refuges and waterfowl production. Not just game birds, but all birds share the benefits."

"I'll never think of duck stamps in quite the same way again," he said lightly.

Tess frowned. "Also the excise tax on guns and ammunition goes for conservation. Prorated to the states, the money enables them to set aside and improve millions of acres for wildlife."

He was impressed by her knowledge. "Wildlife conservation must be pretty important to you."

"Of course. Isn't it to you? I've heard you discuss it on your show. Or was that just more script reading?"

"I'm not an environmental activist, but I know that conservation concerns everyone."

"We face so many shortages—fuel, water, timber, all our natural resources. Like few others, wildlife, if given the proper conditions, will quickly reproduce."

Jack was unable to keep the teasing note from his voice when he said, "I'm glad reproduction is near and dear to your heart."

She ignored the way that comment made her feel and kept to the subject. "Habitat is the key to wildlife survival. It's the animal's environment that supplies everything it needs for life. Food, shelter, water and space."

"I'll be more than happy to give any critter all the space it wants."

She sighed. "I can see you're not in the mood for a serious discussion—"

"On the contrary. I'd seriously like to know more about you."

"You know all you need to know about me. I'm the teacher. What I'm teaching you today are the basics."

"Good. I love the basics."

"Do you also love being a fraud?"

He quickly sobered. "No. But I need to know more about you before we start."

"That isn't necessary. We outfit hundreds of successful hunters every year who do just fine without ever knowing my personal history."

"Don't you have any burning questions you want to ask me?" he persisted.

"What if you don't like my questions?" she queried.

"Hey, I'm an open book. Go ahead, ask anything you want."

"Are you involved in a serious relationship?" She hadn't meant to pose the question so soon, but it had been on her mind.

"No, but I could be persuaded," he said suggestively.

"Well, I can't, and I really don't think I want to get to know you any better than this." Tess stood up and went to the door. "I'm going to check on my father and fix his supper."

Perversely his answer was not the one she'd wanted to hear. His willing availability only made the situation more dangerous. She tried to deny the intensity of their attraction, and when it wouldn't go away, she resented it.

"Don't go," he whispered from right behind her.

Tess's determination crumbled when his fingers stroked the line of her spine through the thick sweater she wore. When he touched her shoulder, she flinched.

"Does it make you crazy when I touch you? It does the strangest things to me," he admitted.

"I wouldn't say *crazy*." The word barely escaped her dry mouth. She felt the warm sliding pressure of his body against hers as his hand followed the outline of her chin, then turned her slightly until their lips nearly touched.

"What about this?" he asked huskily against her mouth as his lips finally settled lightly on her neck.

"Yes," she breathed, and his hand slid beneath her sweater to administer a sensuous massage to her lower back. His lips caressed her cheek then spread their fire to her mouth.

"I've been dying to do this since early this morning," he whispered seductively. "I could almost feel your mouth against mine when I closed my eyes."

The warm nibbling parted her lips, and his tongue swept over the boundary to lightly tease the even line of her teeth, igniting heat waves that spread like wildfire inside her breast. His words made her heart hum with long-repressed need.

The fragrance of him was fresh and piney and as potent to her senses as the outdoors she loved. He cradled her face in his hands, and his lips tasted of coffee and sunshine as they claimed hers. His palms brushed the underside of her chin and gently caressed her neck. Her temperature flared and flooded her with a shuddering heat.

"Should you be standing on that leg?" she whispered.

"Probably not. We could always lie down." He nuzzled her neck. "You're trembling, are you cold?" he murmured as his tongue made a foray around the rim of her ear. His hands slipped down her arms to her waist and pressed her nearer.

"I'll warm you up," he promised when she could not answer. His whisper tickled at her ear.

He'd kissed women before, but Jack had never kissed one so thoroughly in his life. So often kisses were but a prelude, but with Tess he felt no compulsion to hurry on to the next intimate step. Kissing Tess was a main event in itself and he wanted to linger over it and savor each moment.

It was exciting, this feeling of wanting to give, this overpowering need—not for a woman, but for a special woman. Tess was special, and the thought brought discipline to the fire inside him. He enfolded her in his arms, and her face sought the refuge of his chest. He'd known that it would be good; he hadn't expected it to be intense.

He put his hand against the back of her head and stroked the sleek healthy strands of auburn hair. The dying sunlight caught the rich highlights and turned them to flame. Her response told him that he didn't have to stop with a kiss. But that knowledge only made him more protective. No matter how badly he wanted her, he wasn't about to take advantage of her need. Intuition and observation had convinced him that Tess McIver was a lady who needed so much more than she ever asked for.

Jack tipped up her chin and kissed her on the nose. "I think we should stop. I'm a strong guy, but I like where this is going too much."

Disarmed by his sincerity, Tess stepped away from him. "This was a mistake, anyway. I know better than to point a loaded gun." And pointing it at your heart was the most foolhardy thing of all.

Although it was what he wanted, Jack didn't dare take her back into his arms. Not with the desire to make love to her still singing through his body. "I can live with making mistakes, but I can't stand *being* one."

"I'm afraid you are for me," she said shakily as she grabbed her jacket. "I should go." She turned the doorknob before his soft voice stopped her in her tracks.

"Tess?"

"Yes?" She glanced over her shoulder as she wrenched open the door.

"We'll have to talk about this sometime."

"No, we don't."

Jack knew it would be unwise to push her, she wasn't ready. Not yet. "Will you be back later?"

She took several moments to answer, as if she was weighing the question carefully. "No."

"What if my leg starts hurting again?"

"Take two aspirin and call me Monday morning," she said as lightly as she could. Suddenly understanding what it was like to elude a predator, she shut the door between herself and the dangers of Jack Hunter.

"But this is only Saturday. What am I supposed to do until then?" he called after her.

She marched off down the path as though she hadn't heard him. She had her own problems, the biggest of which was the need to build up an immunity to a potentially deadly strain of male charm.

Tess didn't think thirty-six hours would be long enough.

Chapter Five

A number of urgent chores allowed Tess to keep her distance from Cabin Ten and it's disturbing occupant, but Bitterroot seemed determined to make the most of male bonding. He spent the weekend zipping up and down the trail on his three-wheeler, ever ready to swap stories with Hunter or engage their unsuspecting guest in a game of penny-ante poker. As lame as he was, he claimed talking and cards were just about the only pleasures he had left.

Between visits he tried to get Tess to share his enthusiasm about Hunter by endlessly extolling his newly discovered virtues. She wasn't sure how Jack had wormed his way so quickly into her irascible father's affections, but losing consistently at poker hadn't hurt the budding friendship any.

She would have been quite content to leave the two new pals to themselves, but she had a job to do and Monday came all too soon.

When Jack stepped out of his cabin Monday morning, he was overwhelmed by excessive sensory input. The sun was much brighter than in Denver; the air was crisper and heavy with the scent of pine. Billowy clouds drifted like barges in a sky colored the perfect blue of a child's paint box and trailed shadows across the quiet waters of the cove. The lodge, nestled at water's edge in an alpine setting of fairy-tale pines and mystic mountain peaks, looked more like a landscape rendered by an idealistic artist than a creation of man.

Except for the requisite bird song, the morning seemed unnaturally quiet to Jack, whose ears were attuned to the noise of humans and their machines. He'd spent his whole life in cities and understood their rhythms and pace. He thrived on the excitement and had always viewed the world beyond the boulevard as alien territory. What was the challenge of the great outdoors compared to crime and smog and rush hour snarl? Even if they were arbitrary at times, the rules set by society had a comfortable predictability; those set by nature did not.

It was ironic that he'd become the host of an outdoors program. He'd never even been to camp as a kid because his father's job as a factory foreman hadn't covered extras like Camp Hiawatha. The sidewalk was his home. Hunting, fishing and hiking had never rated too highly on his personal thrill scale. He was a night person who preferred sunrises at the end of a wild evening, not at the beginning of a new day.

But now as he limped gingerly down the needle-strewn trail toward the lodge, he was bombarded by nature, and felt the irresistible pull of unspoiled places, places that held a mystique and fascination uniquely their own. For the first time he felt a degree of optimism about the coming month.

Maybe he wouldn't be a true expert at the end of his stay, but he wouldn't be a rank amateur posing as an expert, either. That would make him feel better about himself and the career that had chosen him. According to Norton, those who learned to cherish the natural world had a better perspective of the problems of their own. Learning to be self-reliant, he claimed, was the best way to self-discovery.

None of that had meant much to Jack until now. Maybe if he adopted the right attitude he could learn something about himself this month. And maybe, if he didn't rush into things prematurely, he could learn more about Tess McIver as well.

When he reached the main building, he went around to the kitchen door as Bitterroot had instructed. He knew he was early, but he'd allowed extra time in case his injured leg slowed him down. Feeling surprisingly fit, he decided all the time and money he'd spent at the gym had paid off. He was about to knock when he heard the heated discussion inside.

"You shouldn't have invited him to breakfast, Pop. We're not running a hotel." Tess shoved a pan of sourdough biscuits into the oven.

"Shoot," Bitterroot grumbled. "For what he's payin' us he coulda stayed in a real fancy hotel. He ain't used to so much peace and quiet, and he's been in that cabin alone and fending for himself since Saturday. I was just bein' neighborly."

"He knew the arrangement before he came up here, and he has plenty of food in the cabin."

"I seen all that junk." Bitterroot sat down at the table with a big mug of coffee. "Canned soup, canned meat, canned spaghetti. He even has pudding in a can. The man could end up with lead poisoning eatin' that stuff."

"You never worried about the dietary habits of guests before," she pointed out as she turned a mound of hash brown potatoes sizzling in a cast iron skillet. "Besides, he hasn't had much opportunity to get lonely. You spent all day down there yesterday."

"I didn't bring you up to be unkind, miss." Bitterroot hobbled over to the stove to swipe a piece of bacon from the platter. "What happened between you two anyhow?"

"I filled you in on his medical condition and that's all I have to report," she answered evasively.

"I'm your father and I know when somethin's botherin' you. I have a right to know if he tried anything he shouldn't have."

"I'm twenty-four, Pop. I'm not the same gullible girl who got herself hornswoggled three years ago."

"You ain't no ugly old maid, either," Bitterroot said with a knowing grin.

"Nothing happened. Absolutely nothing." She bustled around, putting the food on the table.

"Come to think of it, Hunter was mighty tight-lipped when I tried to bring your name up." He rubbed his morning stubble thoughtfully. "If he didn't do nothin', how come you flounced in here Saturday evenin' as sore as a frog on a hot skillet?"

"Because he kissed me." The words burst out in a frustrated rush, then Tess's voice softened before she added, "But mainly because I kissed him back."

"You didn't like it, huh?"

She smiled ruefully at her father. "I liked it, all right."

Bitterroot beamed and smacked the table. "Hell's bells, Tessie. That just proves you're human. I was startin' to worry about you after that Dexter fella did what he done."

"Hunter's not like Greg." She had no reason to be so certain, but she was.

"Nope, I reckon he ain't," he conceded.

She looked around to see her father eyeing her speculatively. "Don't go getting any ideas. Even if Jack Hunter is the prince you think he is, he's not for me, so don't even think about matchmaking."

"How come?" Her father snorted. "Somebody's got to."

"We're about as compatible as champagne and trail mix. He's a city person and likes life in the fast lane. I'm a country girl who prefers no lane at all. I get claustrophobia in the city, and he's already got cabin fever from being in the woods two days."

"What's that got to do with the price of beans?"

"I won't be a scalp on another man's belt, Pop. Hunter has an ex-wife to his credit, and I have an even bigger mistake to mine. I won't compound it by getting involved with a man like him.''

"He's only going to be here a month. What harm could come from you lettin' yourself go a little? You never have any fun with people your own age.''

"I know you think I'm being unfair, but I have my reasons.'' Tess finished setting the table, then turned to her father. "For the next twenty-eight days I'll be spending almost every waking moment with Jack. As charming and likable as he can be, I have to keep a distance between us.''

Evidently Bitterroot saw the wisdom in his daughter's words. "We haven't deposited the check, it ain't too late to call the whole thing off.''

"We can't do that, we need the money too much. Jack and I will begin our work today as scheduled.'' And it would definitely be work, for she planned to show him no mercy. "I can handle it.''

"You don't have to if it's gonna cause a problem,'' Bitterroot assured her. "We can get by without that money.''

"Thanks, Pop.'' She dropped a kiss on his white head. "But I have to.''

"If I hadn't fallen through that dad-blamed roof...''

"Nothing happens without a reason. I got us into this financial mess, so it's fitting that I bail us out.''

"All the same I ain't cashin' his check just yet. If you change your mind, you just say the word and we'll send him packin'.''

"I won't change my mind,'' she declared.

"No, I reckon you won't," the old man said lovingly. "You always did like to roll your own hoop."

Jack stood outside and thought about the conversation he'd overheard. Maybe it was true that eavesdroppers never heard anything good about themselves, but they sure learned some interesting things. Tess had confirmed that she was as attracted to him as he was to her. That kiss had meant something to him, and he was glad it had meant something to her.

Knowing she'd been burned emotionally and financially by someone name Greg Dexter gave him a little more insight into Tess's responses. Apparently she considered that, and his own failed marriage, reason enough to deny her feelings. Or maybe she'd been hurt so badly that isolating herself had become a habit. Living way up here, cut off from the larger world, made it easy to do just that.

Jack remembered the protectiveness he'd felt for Tess the morning he'd awakened beside her, and he was filled with a sudden urge to prove to her that all men weren't takers. He knew it was corny, but for some as yet unknown reason, he wanted to be her knight in shining armor. He wanted to be the one who slew her dragons and restored her trust, the one who taught her to love again.

Maybe she could never love him, and maybe they were as unsuitable as she claimed, but he could prove she was wrong about him by overcoming his own fear of discomfort and ridicule. His success this month would show her that nothing worthwhile was without risk, and perhaps it would make her give life another chance. It was a formidable task, and considering the start he'd made, he had to wonder if he was up to it.

Before he lost his zeal for challenge, Jack pounded on the door as if he'd just arrived.

The first lesson of the day was fishing, and after a lumberjack's breakfast, Jack went to his cabin to fetch the equipment he'd brought along. When he returned, he parked near the dock and started unloading his car.

From her perch on a piling, Tess watched in amused amazement as the stack grew until it rivaled the inventory of a medium-size sporting goods store.

He might be a novice, she mused, but like a true actor, he was dressed for the part. His pale orange jumpsuit sported a dozen zippered pockets and manufacturer patches. His name was embroidered in fancy script over his heart. He wore a pair of wraparound, guaranteed-to-see-through-the-water polarizing sunglasses and authorized boating shoes.

"Hey, Tess," he called. "Would you come over here and help me select what I'll need?"

She sauntered across the dock and looked over the choices. There were half a dozen fishing rods ranging in length from three to nine feet, most with the price tags still hanging from them.

"I know I don't need them all, but you didn't say what we'd be fishing for today and I wanted to be prepared for anything," he explained when he saw her expression.

"Where did you get all this stuff?"

"The prop room. Norton boxed it up for me."

"And the outfit?" she asked with a barely concealed grin.

"Manufacturers send us their products hoping we'll use them on the show." Maybe the jumpsuit was too much. Tess was dressed far more comfortably. And provocatively. Her khaki shorts emphasized her long, sleek legs and trim waist. The white T-shirt, emblazoned with the slogan Hooked on Fishing, clung to her well-endowed chest and reminded him of far more interesting sports they could engage in.

Banishing such troublesome thoughts, he plucked a cap from the pile and put it on. "Norton wears his cap backward. Why do fishermen wear them that way? Is it part of some obscure fishing ritual?"

"Beats me." Tess grabbed her own well-worn cap, on which a number of colorful flies were pinned. "I wear mine to keep the sun out of my eyes."

"So what should I take?" Last night's reading had concentrated more on technique than on equipment, but he'd soon decided that where fishing was concerned, book learning was about as effective as a correspondence course in diesel truck driving.

"We're going after trout so you'll need a fly rod." She looked over the assortment and chose a rod and casting reel. "These should do it. I have the flies."

Jack pulled out an expensive pair of waders. "I hope these are all right." He hadn't even been sure what they were until he'd verified it by reading the accompanying instruction booklet.

"Have you used waders before?" Tess asked uncertainly.

"No."

"They can be dangerous if used improperly," she warned.

He recalled that much from the chapters on safety. He'd been especially interested in that aspect of the sport. "I read up on the subject and I know what I'm doing." He sounded more confident than he felt, but he was appalled by the thought of standing in the lake without something between him and whatever lurked beneath the surface.

Tess knew she should advise him against the waders until he became more adept at fishing, but some perverse streak kept her from doing so. She would let him see for himself how clumsy they could be for novices.

When Jack tugged on the last of his gear, he turned to see Tess loading the rest of his things into a small rowboat. Rowing. Now there was something he could do.

"Take a seat up front," she instructed, "and put this on." She tossed him an orange life preserver before buckling on her own.

Dressed as he was, Jack already felt foolish and was irritated by the order. "I don't need one. I'm an excellent swimmer. And I insist on rowing the boat. I was captain of the rowing team in college."

"Good for you. But I'd rather do it myself. I know where we're going." Tess slipped the oars into the water and rowed leisurely out of the cove.

A natural lake, the Big Bear was nothing like the expansive artificial reservoirs created by dams. Composed of a series of quiet inlets and coves, it was fed by fast-moving streams carrying runoff water from the higher elevations. Pine-covered islands had been created when the water had chosen the path of least resistance. The lake was home to a variety of game fish, including their quarry for the day—brown trout.

"I feel kind of stupid sitting here while you do all the work," Jack grumbled after a while. Although he did enjoy watching her fluid movements. She handled the oars with ease, her sleekly muscled arms pushing and pulling them rhythmically through the water.

"Why don't you use the time constructively by reading that handbook you stashed in your tackle box," she suggested with a grin.

He'd hoped she hadn't seen that, and looked embarrassed.

In an attempt to ease the strain between them, she said, "There's no shame in being a beginner, Jack. Not even the experts learned it in the womb."

There was no sarcasm in her tone this time and he smiled gratefully before flipping through the handbook. After a few minutes he closed it. "This is confusing. Why don't you explain it to me in terms I can understand?" He'd rather concentrate on Tess than on dry text any day.

She guided the boat into a secluded area of the lake. "The first thing you need to know is that fly fishing differs from rod-and-reel angling because you cast the line, not the lure. The flies are attached by an almost invisible leader to the fly line. They're practically weightless and are designed to imitate insects. Wet flies sink below the surface and dry flies dance on top. Any questions so far?"

"Yeah. What's the point of fishing?" Jack had never understood the fascination the sport held for some people.

Tess laughed. "Catching fish, of course. There's no better eating in the world than trout panfried only hours out of the water."

"That's it? Food?" he asked in amazement. "People spend hundreds of dollars on equipment and years perfecting technique for food?"

"Well, yes."

"This may sound simplistic, but wouldn't a restaurant be a better bet for that?"

She laughed again, unsure if he was kidding or not. "Sure. But fishing nourishes the spirit because it provides an excuse to sit in a boat in the middle of a lake and dream. If the fish are striking, good. If not, you can enjoy the scenery. You can relax, reflect and do nothing. Few people take the time anymore to do nothing."

Jack considered his own hectic schedule. In his goal-oriented world, doing nothing was considered a capital crime. To Tess it was gainful employment. "I'll try to keep all that in mind." He eyed their surroundings skeptically. They'd slipped into a narrow inlet where the pine trees crowded down to water's edge and cast deep shadows on the surface.

Due to a lifelong, albeit irrational, fear of reptiles, Jack decided a question was in order. "Are there any snakes around here?"

"Probably. I think I see one across the lake right now." Tess stopped rowing and pointed. "See?"

He gazed in that direction. "Looks like a big twig to me," he said hopefully.

"You could be right, it's hard to tell from this distance." She pulled the oars inside and dropped a small anchor. "Don't worry, the water isn't deep here. About the only time to be afraid of water snakes is when they've formed a ball. Balls of snakes are usually only found in deep water."

He was dubious. The natural debris and partially submerged tree trunks seemed like perfect hiding places for the sneaky creatures. "Won't casting be a problem in here?"

"You can avoid hangups by steering the lure around obstacles. That in itself can be a lot of fun."

"Right." Fun? "I'm not concerned with having fun, I just want to be successful."

"Out you go," she said cheerfully.

Yuck. Jack resisted the urge to mutter the word aloud as he regarded the aquatic minefield of lily pads, stumps and floating sticks. Silently he thanked Norton for the waders. With a good deal of trepidation, he cautiously slid first one leg, then the other, over the side until he was hip deep in the water.

"Now what, boss?" he said in a tone that he hoped conveyed the right amount of nonchalance.

"Let the fishing begin," she said, her lips twitching as she handed him his rod and reel.

"Aren't you joining me?"

"I'll instruct you from here. Try casting toward the bank so I can see your technique."

What technique? Jack mentally reviewed the steps to a successful cast and sent the fly spinning out over the water. It was a lousy attempt and he knew it. He'd seen experts do it and realized it was a lot harder than it looked. He reeled in the line to try again.

"Don't hurl your arm," Tess reprimanded. "It's a fly, not a baseball."

He tried again. And again and again. Finally, when his arm was nearly paralyzed from the effort, Tess was satisfied.

"Okay, I think you're ready."

"Ready and willing," he said with a wink. She'd been all business, but he couldn't stop thinking about the kiss they'd shared, longing for another one.

"Just go for it."

"I thought you'd never ask." He grinned roguishly and waded toward her. "Are you sure it's wise to try something so physical on a boat?"

Tess rolled her eyes. She'd been waiting for him to do what he did best—read something sexual into an innocent comment. She ignored him. "Get out there and start casting. You don't get back in this boat without a trout."

Jack laughed good-naturedly. "The proverbial hell could freeze over before that happens."

"Not with your determination. And mine. Get back over there where I showed you."

"Okay, okay." Jack gamely waded back in the other direction. He'd best keep his mind on his goal. Judging from the position of the sun he only had about nine or ten hours left before nightfall.

Tess called out directions and Jack worked the line for half an hour before he became bored with the uneventful sport. Patience had never been his strong suit, and fishing required it. "How long do I have to keep this up?"

"We can't move on until you've perfected it," she intoned.

When concentration didn't pay off, he tried to take Tess's advice and daydream. But that only got him in trouble when they turned into uncomfortable fantasies involving a certain auburn-haired guide.

"I'm hungry," he complained.

"We had breakfast less than two hours ago," she reminded him.

"My leg is getting pretty tired," he grumbled as he cast again.

"The water's good for it. Now, try to use less wrist action."

His next attempt was more successful, but when he tugged, the lure disappeared under the water. Jack pulled harder.

"Don't pull on it," she directed. "It's snagged."

"No kidding. So, what do I do now?"

"Wade over there and untangle it, of course."

"Figures," he muttered. Flotsam, and lots of it, made him cautious. The thought of what might be lurking beneath it sent his vivid imagination swirling. He'd taken only a few steps into the weedy patch where his fly had disappeared, when he stumbled on a large rock.

A black, ropey thing bobbed to the surface a few feet away and his worst fears were confirmed.

"Snake!" He backed away from the knobby-looking head, then turned and headed clumsily for the relative safety of the boat. Movement was difficult in the heavy waders, and the resistance of the water hurt his injured thigh. He glanced over his shoulder to see if the snake was gaining on him.

When it seemed he might reach the boat before the snake reached him, his reel ran out of line and the rod was nearly jerked from his hand. His feet were still slogging forward but the upper portion of his body was violently stopped short, causing him to lose his balance. He tumbled backward into the water.

"Be careful of those waders, Jack," Tess called to him as he went under. She hoisted the anchor and rowed over in case he needed help.

When he surfaced he saw her grinning at him.

"What's so damn funny?" he demanded. "I could get bitten before I get into the boat, you know."

"By a stick?" she asked incredulously. "I'm sorry, but when I saw you trying to hurry in those waders... and I knew it wasn't a snake..." She dissolved into another fit of giggles.

Jack grinned at the silly picture he must have presented. "You have a warped sense of humor." He tried to lift his bad leg over the side of the boat but his waders had filled with water and the soreness from his injury made it impossible.

"I can't get these damn things off. This is all your fault."

"I know." Tess lowered herself into the water. "But the best lessons are those learned by mistake."

"Still, you should have been more specific."

"Yes, I should have," she agreed solemnly.

"Let's compromise. I'll promise to listen to you if you promise to sound a little less like a Marine drill sergeant."

"Deal." Tess took the hand he offered and shook it before helping him out of his water-filled waders. "Seems like I'm forever having to undress you, doesn't it?" she asked with an ornery grin.

"That's been the highlight of my trip so far." He put his hands on her shoulders. "Maybe when you've perfected the technique, we can move on."

Despite her good intentions, Tess was drawn to Jack. She strained imperceptively toward him, the memory of his kiss potent in her mind. How easy he made her forget her inhibitions by reducing everything to its most elemental level. How simple it would be to wrap her arms around his neck and kiss him until the longing was satisfied.

Instead she moved away from him. "I'll take you back to the lodge so you can change into dry clothing."

After being foiled by a floating twig, Jack was compelled to redeem a measure of his self-esteem. He moved his hands to her waist and lifted her up into the boat. "I thought I had to catch a fish first."

At that moment the sound of a revving motor directed their attention to an approaching boat. The occupant took time out from snapping photos to wave, then motored over beside them.

"Who's that?" Jack muttered as he climbed in the boat.

Tess squinted in the sun. "I think it's a little old lady I met at the hospital. Be nice, she thinks we're newlyweds."

Maddie steered up beside them and cut her engine. "Tess! Fancy meeting you like this." Her wig had been dislodged by the wind and she tugged it into place.

"Hello, Mrs. Flame," Tess greeted. "This is quite a surprise."

"Call me Maddie, dear. I was hiking on the other side of the lake, and it was such a lovely day I decided to do something impulsive. So I rented this boat. It's been years since I've done anything so exhilarating." She took a breath and added, "Aren't you going to introduce me to your husband, dear?"

"Of course. This is Jack."

The three exchanged pleasantries before Maddie observed, "I couldn't help noticing that you seemed to be in trouble."

Jack's laugh was forced. "We were just horsing around." He put his arm around Tess's shoulder and smiled down at her. "Tessie likes to be playful. Don't you, honey?"

She nodded and put her arm around Jack's waist so she could pinch him without being detected.

Maddie smiled. "You two make such a handsome couple. You're both so tall and athletic. You're sure to have beautiful children." She focused her expensive camera, and the motor drive whirred away. "If you'll give me your address, I'll see that you get these pix."

Reluctantly Tess gave it to her. "I'm glad you've recovered from your emergency, whatever it was,

Jack," the older woman said in a tone that clearly begged for more information.

He wasn't about to give any. "Yes, thank you."

"I guess I've intruded on you two long enough, I know how honeymoon couples enjoy their privacy. I only rented the boat for an hour so I'd best not dawdle." She raced the engine as she waved goodbye. "I'll be seeing you," she called over the roar as she sped out of the cove.

"Not if we see you first," Jack said cheerfully.

"That's not nice." Tess wriggled out of his embrace.

He frowned. "I don't buy it."

"Buy what?"

"I don't believe that woman just *happened* to find us on this great big lake. Little old ladies don't have cameras like that. That's a professional model."

"Maybe photography is her hobby. For goodness sakes, she's just a lonely old lady."

"She was wearing a disguise. That wig is a dead giveaway."

"The hair underneath it is gray. Maybe she's a vain little old lady who likes nature photography." Tess didn't know why she was defending the woman, but she seemed harmless enough.

"And that name! Madelyn Flame sounds like a stripper. Or a byline."

"A reporter? Maddie?"

Jack shook his head. "She's a phony if I ever saw one."

"You should know. You see one every time you look in the mirror," she challenged.

"Never mind." He was too tired to try and change her mind. "Let's get on with the fishing."

Tess seated herself and took up the oars, deciding she'd spent enough time in his company for one day. "We're heading back."

"I still haven't caught any fish," he argued, unwilling to give up.

"We'll try again after lunch," she said, pulling rank.

She might be the boss, but Jack wasn't about to be relegated into another submissive position today. He stood towering over her "Have it your way. But this time, I'll do the rowing."

She could tell by the look on his face that he wouldn't take no for an answer. "Fine."

"Good."

She stood and scrambled to the front of the boat. Without the anchor to secure it, the small craft lurched in the water.

"Be careful, Tess. You're rocking the boat."

Chapter Six

Bitterroot was waiting for them on the dock when they returned to the lodge for lunch. Tess tossed her father the line and he secured the boat. "Catch anything?" he asked.

She shook her head and he extended his hand and pulled her onto the dock. "Then I reckon it's a good thing I made stew."

"What's up, Pop? You didn't come all the way down here to tell us about the soup of the day."

"I wanted to catch Jack before he went up to the cabin." He scratched his chin thoughtfully. "I might have some bad news."

"What is it?" Jack asked.

"Might be somethin', might be nothin'," the old man said cryptically. "I'll tell you after we have a bite to eat." He limped to his three-wheeler and sped away in a cloud of dust.

"I hate it when he does that," Tess muttered. "He likes to withhold information until the setting is perfect."

"I think he just likes to feel needed," Jack observed. "That can be pretty difficult around you." Without giving her a chance to respond, he started for the lodge.

Bitterroot had prepared his specialty—meatball stew and cornbread. As usual when he cooked, the kitchen was a shambles, but Tess appreciated the gesture and the hot meal.

She dished up the food, still fuming over Jack's last remark. He offered no further explanation, and pride would not allow her to press for one. There was nothing wrong with being self-sufficient. She'd learned the hard way not to trust her happiness and well-being to a man. The more you needed someone, the greater the potential for pain.

Since such thoughts were more suitable for solitary reflection, Tess sat down to eat and prodded Bitterroot. "Aren't you going to tell us the news?"

The old man frowned. "Jack, you said no one knows where you are, right?"

"Only Norton, but he wouldn't tell anyone. Why?"

"I got a call from one of them reporter fellas this mornin'. He said he'd heard you was here and wanted to book a cabin so he could come and interview you. When I told him we were closed to guests, he offered to make it worth my while. I told him no and hung up."

"Then there's nothing to worry about," Tess said, relieved. Without realizing it, she had feared Jack might have been called back to Denver. She told herself she was worried about losing the training fee, but she knew there was another, more personal reason.

"I hope not," Jack agreed. "But those media types are relentless when they smell a kill. I don't think it's a coincidence that you ran into Maddie at the hospital or that she came nosing around this morning, Tess."

"Who's Maddie?" Bitterroot asked, clearly perplexed.

"You think Maddie leaked something to the press?" Tess asked.

"Maybe she *is* the press," Jack stressed.

"That's ridiculous. Maddie thinks your name is Jack *McIver*."

Bitterroot looked first at Tess, then at Jack. "Who's Maddie?"

"Maddie is not what she seems," Jack insisted.

Tess folded her arms and glared at him. "You're impossible. Just because you pass yourself off as someone you're not, you assume the worst of everyone you meet."

Bitterroot's soup spoon stopped midway to his mouth. "Whoa there! What do you mean Jack McIver?" When no one would answer him, he sagged back in his chair.

Jack chewed his stew furiously and swallowed hard before addressing Tess. "I know how hard it is for a straight arrow like you to accept less than perfection in others."

Bitterroot watched the heated exchange like a spectator at a tennis match. "What is goin' on here?"

Jack scraped his chair back from the table, grabbed some cornbread and picked up his bowl. "I'm going outside where I can eat in peace."

"You just do that," Tess snapped.

"When you're ready to resume fishing lessons, let me know." Then he added scathingly, *"Boss."*

When the back door slammed shut behind him, Bitterroot pounded his fist on the table. "Hell's bells, Tess. Will you please tell me who this Maddie person is and why she thinks Jack's name is *McIver?*"

Two hours later the erstwhile anglers were back in the cove, and Jack was learning to troll with bait-fish lures. Falling into the rhythm of the lake, he closed his eyes for a moment and focused on the soothing noise of the woodland. Water lapped against the bank where a woodpecker tapped busily in a tree. A soft breeze played among the branches, and across the lake a wild duck quacked and a boat engine roared.

The day was filled with sounds, but the one thing he wasn't likely to hear was Tess's voice. She wasn't speaking to him.

He opened his eyes and noticed a phalanx of gray clouds moving in over the mountains. They were bringing a summer storm; he could almost smell the rain. He glanced up to see if Tess had noticed, but she was too busy catching fish to worry about weather conditions. Except for issuing orders and clipping instructions, she'd scarcely spoken since lunch, and the silent treatment was wearing on his nerves.

"This is getting us nowhere," he said, referring to her obstinate behavior.

"Then stop trolling and try these weighted nymphs." Tess handed him a bunch of strange-looking lures. "They're working fine for me."

When he cast, the heavy lure struck his shoulder with a forceful splat and the hook caught in the fishing vest that had replaced the coveralls. "It's stuck. Would you mind getting it out?"

With the forbearance of a fishing instructor who'd seen it all, Tess put down her rod and inched to the front of the boat. She worked the fly free and dropped it into his palm. Then she dusted her hands on the seat of her shorts and went back to her perch. She picked up her rod and calmly cast toward the bank, tugged on the line and netted another trout.

"Why can't I do that?" Jack asked impatiently as she stowed the fish in the cooler.

She shrugged. "Fishing is an iffy business. But your casting has improved dramatically since this morning. Keep trying."

Jack was astounded. Had he detected a word of praise in there somewhere? Coming from Tess it was hard to tell. "Maybe you've already caught all the fish around here," he grumbled. He cast again, and again the fly snagged in his vest. "Damn!"

Tess sighed and went forward to remove it. "Don't give up. Somewhere down there, there's a trout with your name on it."

"I hope it likes big weighted nymphs," he said sourly. He succeeded on his next attempt and the fly painted a parallel stroke along the bottom, where an unsuspecting trout could plainly see it. He expected to see the lure tumbling toward him, when surprisingly, the line fought back.

He set the hook and tugged. "I got one!" Despite his excitement, he did everything right. He pulled his rod tip up, took the slack out of the line and eased up the pressure on the fish.

Tess netted the four-pound beauty and held it high. "You did good, Jack."

His enthusiasm over his first catch set the boat rocking, tipping it first one way and then the other. Tess clutched the sides, but before she could call out a warning, the motion spilled Jack into the drink.

One moment he was admiring his fish, and the next he was sitting in the water. He looked up to see Tess laughing. Scrambling to his feet, he jitterbugged around in the shallows before extracting a small trout from inside his shirt. When she saw the fish he was waving, Tess laughed harder.

"Two," he spluttered. "Baby makes two."

"Not bad for a beginner his first day out," she told him.

He dropped the fingerling back into the water and stood up. Before he could get in the boat, he heard a crashing sound in the bushes along the bank. "What was that?"

"Probably an animal you disturbed with all that splashing around."

"It must be a pretty big animal to make that much noise. Do you get many bears around here?"

"A few. Whatever it was, it's gone now."

Jack climbed back into the boat and picked up his rod. "Keep that net ready," he said with a determined look. "I think my luck has changed."

And so it had. By the time the rain came and forced them homeward, he'd added a considerable number of trout to Tess's cooler. Her praise was genuine but grudging, and Jack suspected her expectations had been disappointed. The fact that he wasn't totally hopeless meant that she might have to revise her initial opinion of him. And Tess hated to admit she was wrong.

He knew one bountiful afternoon did not a seasoned angler make, but he was encouraged by his success—and by the fact that he had actually *enjoyed* fishing once he'd had a real taste of the sport.

His enthusiasm seemed to dispel Tess's bad mood and in turn, his own. She promised to show him how to clean, fillet and cook their catch. After supper he anticipated sitting in front of a nice warm fire at the lodge. Maybe if his luck held, she would open up to him a little. As frustrating as she could be at times, he was no less intrigued by her. Tess McIver was a puzzle with no easy solution.

Back at the lodge, they ran up to the covered porch and stood there watching the rain pelt down. What had started as a soft drizzle had grown to a downpour that had drenched them both. Tess felt Jack's gaze on her wet T-shirt and it seemed to burn through the thin material. She folded her arms over her chest, but the action only pushed her breasts up provocatively. He stepped close, his eyes now trained on hers. Something inside her responded to his frightening intensity, and her breath caught in her throat.

"I don't think—" she began.

"That's right." He tilted up her chin. With his free hand he brushed the damp hair away from her face and stroked her cheek. "Don't think, Tess. Just do." His lips descended and she felt herself tumbling toward disaster.

All afternoon she'd pretended to concentrate on fishing when in reality nothing had been farther from her mind. All she could think of was the man in her boat and the way his kisses and big warm body made her feel. Such thoughts weren't normal for her, and that preoccupation worried her.

Since Greg, she'd hardened her heart against men. Maybe it wasn't fair to judge them all by the deeds of one, but she'd done so out of self-preservation. Male guests of all ages and charm levels thronged regularly to the lodge. Her work required her to be a pal to them without giving them any encouragement. The hands-off manner she'd perfected had served her well.

But hard-won objectivity was failing her now, she realized, as Jack kissed his way across her face. She knew what he was and yet she'd allowed him to draw her into a dangerous realm of unexplored emotions. She had sworn never to be suckered by another pretty line, and yet she was willing to surrender to sensation at his touch. One kiss and she'd be a goner. With Jack she couldn't be rational . . . she couldn't deny.

Bitterroot opened the door and broke the spell just as Jack's lips found Tess's. The old man looked embarrassed and flustered when he saw their embrace.

"Uh, sorry. I thought I heard someone out here." Then he whispered fiercely, "You best come in. We got company."

The dithery Maddie Flame appeared at Bitterroot's side and hooked her arm in his. After explaining how curiosity about the lodge had led her there, she gushed, "Tess, shame on you for not telling me about your handsome father-in-law."

Because Tess had filled him in earlier, Bitterroot had obviously played along with Maddie's mistaken assumption that Jack was his son. How she wished this tangle of lies had never gotten started. At moments like this it was hard to remember when her life had not been complicated by the presence of Jack Hunter.

Jack forced a laugh and hugged her. "Everything's so new to us, she probably just forgot. Right, darling?"

"Right, precious," she ground out.

He frowned and whispered, "Try to sound more sincere, sweetheart."

Tess muttered behind her hand, "I think it's time to tell the truth, *honey.*"

"You're the one who started this," he hissed. "We can't stop now."

Maddie laughed. "Isn't love grand? You're so cute, sharing your little secrets. It brings back memories of sweeter times, doesn't it Bitterroot?" she asked.

"No," the old man exclaimed as he untangled his arm from the wily lady who'd commandeered it. "I think they should wait until they're alone for that stuff."

Knowing he would never be permitted such liberties in private, Jack patted Tess's backside as she preceded him inside. The familiarity earned him a stabbing look, but it was worth it.

In an apparent effort to ease the tension, Bitterroot lifted the lid of the cooler and whistled appreciatively. "Look at all them fish, will you? You catch any, Jack?"

"Only about half."

Only about half. Tess rolled her eyes at his self-effacing modesty.

"My, my, aren't they lovely? It's been ages since I've eaten freshly caught trout," Maddie hinted broadly.

"Why don't you stay for supper," Tess invited, despite matching glares from Jack and her father. "We have plenty."

Maddie smiled coyly. "How kind of you. I believe I'll accept your generous invitation. Normally I wouldn't think of intruding, but I hate the thought of driving home until this rain lets up."

After supper Bitterroot excused himself on urgent business and left the young people to see Maddie to her car, a dilapidated Volkswagen Beetle that had probably rolled off the assembly line the same year she got her driver's license. Jack gazed after it thoughtfully as she drove away.

"I can't figure out why she really showed up here today."

"She's just a lonely old lady, Jack. Why else would she go to so much trouble?"

"Why indeed? I think she knows we were lying to her and was trying to trip us up. I caught her taking notes when our backs were turned."

"What are you getting at?"

"I think she's a reporter bent on exposing me to the world."

"I think you're being paranoid. Maddie may be nosy, but I hardly think she has ulterior motives."

"I hope you're right," he said grimly.

It rained off and on for the next few days, but that didn't stop Tess from proceeding with the next round of lessons—backpacking, or as Jack had once heard it referred to, misery in all its glory.

When he grumbled about rising at dawn for day hikes, Tess banged on his door even earlier. When he complained about the mud and the insects, she turned a deaf ear. When he griped about the trail rations, she packed no rations at all and taught him to forage for roots and berries. One breakfast of tree bark and slimy little mushrooms was enough to make him a lifelong devotee of granola bars.

In spite of his initial lack of enthusiasm for the sport, Jack was a surprisingly quick study. Because Tess's educational motto was Actions Speak Louder Than Words, she made him do things over and over, until he could accomplish most tasks in the dark. He soon mastered the basics of roughing it, including campsite selection, fire building, latrine digging and shelter erection.

During their day hikes in the forest, he learned to recognize animal signs, and Tess shared her extensive knowledge of plant life. Not only did he develop a healthy respect for nature, but his self-confidence received a much-needed boost. As Tess pointed out, the world situation was so uncertain that the day might come when those who could find their own food and live without electric conveniences would be the only survivors.

In the woods behind the lodge, she taught him to cook with little more than sticks and stones and tin cans. He fried eggs on rocks, started sourdough and baked biscuits in a Dutch oven. He cooked fish on a spit and chicken in a pit. Around a companionable evening campfire, Tess and Bitterroot introduced him to the joy of that old campers' standby—s'mores. And after a long day slogging over a mountain with a forty-pound pack on his back, those ashen marshmallows and gooey chocolate bars squashed between graham crackers were as delicious to Jack as fine French pastry.

Tess was impressed by his progress. What he lacked in skill, he made up for in stubborn determination. From what she knew of Jack, she surmised that things had always come easy for him. No doubt he'd gotten by on charm and good looks most of his life, but she sensed untapped strength in his character. A resourcefulness that had never been challenged before. She wanted him to know the powerful sense of accomplishment that came from tackling a difficult goal and reaching it. So she pushed him relentlessly, never willing to accept less than his best effort.

He frequently rebelled against her authority, but he understood his limitations and deferred to her experience in the end. Men often came to the lodge with a bad case of he-manitis and thought they should already know everything there was to know about the outdoors simply because they were men. But Jack, who knew he was a tenderfoot, was secure enough in his masculinity not to suffer from that particular complex.

All during that rainy week, their confrontations tested their humor, perseverance and commitment, but at the end of it, Tess generously admitted that Jack was doing far better than she'd ever dared hope.

But that was the extent of her largess. Despite her growing attraction to him, she wasn't about to let him know how hard it was to resist his constant teasing and flirting. Nor could she tell him that she found his earnestness almost endearing.

Those feelings confused her. She could survive in the woods alone, with nothing more than her wits. But she wasn't sure her heart could survive Jack Hunter. He was physically appealing and possessed a pistol-quick wit. He didn't hesitate to turn his sense of humor on himself if he thought it would make her laugh.

He was never mean or cruel and was incredibly optimistic that he would ultimately succeed in everything he set out to do. Once she learned not to take his sexual overtures seriously, she realized what good company he was. She also realized just how empty her own life had been for the past few years.

She admired Jack, but she was still determined not to let anything physical damage their working relationship. His pride was dependent on him becoming the best outdoorsman she could make him in thirty

short days. She demanded his best. She owed him
hers.

She was willing, however, to take her father's advice and enjoy herself a little. Which wasn't at all hard
to do with Jack.

On the very next sunny day they met at the archery
range so she could introduce him to the shooting
sports. She pinned a paper target on a thick round of
straw and handed him a bow and arrow.

"Have you ever used a compound bow?" she asked.

"Aside from little boy Indian raids, I've never used
any bow." He examined the strange-looking device
with its many strings and pulleys.

"Bow hunting and competitive archery are more
popular every year. The compound bow makes the
sport accessible because it was designed to reduce the
amount of muscle power required to hold the bowstring back at full force. They're especially good for
women and children whose upper body strength isn't
as great as a man's. Since you don't have to worry
about the strength factor you may want to try a conventional bow once you've mastered the art."

"Norton mentioned having a show next season
featuring archery," Jack told her.

"Good. By the time I'm through with you, you can
do your own shooting and they won't have to call in
Robin Hood to stand in for you."

She showed him how to brace his feet, how to position his body, how to hold the bow. Close bodily
contact was unavoidable during such demonstra-
tions, but she tried not to notice the woodsy tang of his
after-shave, or the minty warmth of his breath. She'd

walked many men through the graceful movements of archery, but their nearness had never made her heart race or her mouth go dry.

She corrected Jack's execution, and the movement was almost an embrace. "I like archery better than fishing," he announced in a teasing voice. "It isn't as lonely."

Tess stepped away from him and showed him how to nock an arrow in the bowstring. "Pay attention," she chided as she taught him the correct way to draw back the string. "When you feel ready, let it fly."

The string zinged when he released the arrow and the colorful shaft skimmed through the air toward the target. It struck the straw bale but missed the paper target by several inches.

"Let me try again." Jack plucked another arrow from the leather quiver. He made a few minor adjustments in balance and this time the tip barely grazed the paper. "I'm getting closer," he said resolutely as he sent arrow after arrow flying toward the bull's-eye.

Tess watched Jack's determined efforts with amusement. Bitterroot had presented her with her first archery equipment when she was seven. Not toys, but a child-size hand-carved bow, and arrows he had fletched himself. On a late-summer day much like this one, he'd patiently taught her the secrets of the primitive weapon. She'd been just as eager to perfect her skill as Jack was now. Like him, she'd run back and forth between the target and the shooting line, releasing and retrieving arrows until she'd been ready to drop from exhaustion.

She'd refused to stop until she hit a bull's-eye, and it wasn't until late that evening, when the sun was almost gone, that she made it. Since then she'd become an accomplished archer who often competed in local matches. But no success was as sweet as that first bull's-eye, and she wanted Jack to experience the feeling.

It took all afternoon.

"Bull's-eye!" he finally yelled. They walked to the target together to examine the hit. When he started to pull out the arrow, Tess stopped him.

"Leave it. Now go back to the shooting line and put ten more right beside it."

Jack was disappointed by her attitude and stalked angrily back to his position. His arms fairly trembled from exertion, his back hurt and his knees were weak. For hours he'd been shooting at that stupid target, and she wouldn't even acknowledge his effort. She stood coolly off to the side, her arms folded, waiting for the impossible.

Eleven bull's-eyes in a row! The woman was a sadist. Worse, she wanted him to fail. Well, he wouldn't do it. He'd show her Jack Hunter was no flash in the pan.

He nocked another arrow and concentrated as he released it to the wind. It thunked in beside the first. A strange new excitement mounted inside him and the sweat of self-imposed pressure beaded on his forehead. He shot again and again, each arrow miraculously joining its fellows in the little red circle.

Filled with an astounding sense of accomplishment, he didn't stop with eleven. He kept shooting until there was no more room in the inner circle.

"There," he challenged Tess fiercely. "Are you satisfied?"

She smiled knowingly. "Are you?"

"Hell, yes." He was confused. Why did she look so pleased if she'd set him up to fail?

"Good. I knew you could do it, but I wanted you to know it, too. You should be proud of yourself. I am." She walked to the target and started pulling the arrows out.

Understanding dawned, and he realized that she'd only wanted him to feel confident about his ability. One bull's-eye could be attributed to luck. Thirteen in a row could only be skill.

"Tess?" He stepped up behind her and turned her into his arms.

"Yes, Jack?" Her heart pounded at his touch.

"Thank you. For everything. You've given me so much in the week I've been here. And you don't even like me."

"I like you," she said softly.

He kissed her then, a long, lingering, blood-stirring kiss that was like being caught in a buffeting wind. Her dormant senses responded with alarming intensity to his kiss, his touch. She clung to him in the waning sunlight and a delicate thread of desire began to weave them together.

Chapter Seven

Tess drew away from Jack's embrace and tried to reorient herself to the real world. What had she been thinking of?

"Don't push me away, Tess," he murmured.

"Stop," she breathed. She attempted to slip out of his arms but he held fast. "Please, Jack. We can't let this get out of hand. I have a job to do and I can't afford to get emotionally involved with you."

He tilted her chin up, forcing her to look at him. "Is that what I am to you, a job?"

She wanted to say yes, but the word wouldn't come and he pressed on. "Did you mean it when you said you were proud of me?"

When she nodded, he added, "I'm glad. Your opinion is very important."

She looked at him in surprise. "Why?"

"I don't know," he replied honestly. "That's part of my confusion. I wish I understood what's happening here, but I don't."

"Nothing's happening." Tess had to get away from his intoxicating nearness. She squeezed past him and hurried to the shooting line to gather up the equipment. When he followed, she added, "Maybe we shouldn't analyze everything. Maybe we should just chalk it up to temporary insanity. Or hormones. You're a man who's used to a lot of female adoration—I'm the only female available. I spend a lot of time in the woods alone—I got caught up in your charm. It's really not so hard to understand," she said flippantly.

"Charm?" Jack helped her stuff the arrows into the quiver. "For your information, we shared something special with that kiss."

Tess wanted to tell him how much it had meant to her, but she knew better than to open that line of discussion. It was too dangerous. Jack was a temporary distraction. In a few weeks he would go back to his glamorous life and never think about her again. She couldn't let him know how important he was becoming to her.

"Look, Jack, let's not make a big deal out of this. You kissed me and I won't deny that I liked it, but it can't happen again. I'm here to get you out of a jam, not to be a pleasant diversion. If we get sidetracked by a lot of mushy stuff, you'll never be ready for the show in time."

The way she said it hurt as much as the words. How could she refer to the magic that happened when they kissed as "a lot of mushy stuff"? He knew what she was doing. She was denying reality. She liked being in control, and she couldn't control what happened when he kissed her. Well, if it comforted her to think it wouldn't happen again, she was welcome to the silly notion. He wouldn't press her now, but neither would he make any promises.

"And a fine job you're doing, too." He couldn't keep his irritation from showing. "After a week of tromping around in the woods, I know which berries to eat and which ones to stay away from. I've learned that tree bark is only slightly less appetizing than dehydrated chicken. I know how to avoid poison ivy, poison oak and poison sumac, as well as what to do in case of snakebite, hypothermia, and heatstroke."

"You catch on fast."

"You didn't think I would."

"I never said that."

"You didn't have to," he said softly. "I see it in your eyes every time I make a blunder."

"What do you see in my eyes when you succeed?" she countered.

"In a word? Astonishment." He laughed and so did she. "What do I have to do to prove myself to you, Tess McIver?"

It was past suppertime and she turned and started back to the lodge. "Just keep your end of the bargain. And let me keep mine."

Several days later, after an intensive review of gun safety and handling, Tess deemed Jack ready for shooting lessons. Careful not to bring up the embarrassing memory of his earlier misuse of weapons, she took him to the firing range behind the lodge and started to explain the differences between the rifles arrayed on a rustic table.

"I know all this already."

"You do?"

"What do you think I've been doing all these long, lonely evenings?"

She shrugged as if the thought of what he did or didn't do never crossed her mind.

"I've been studying. Rifles are named by caliber. This is a .22. The caliber is the measured distance from the top of one groove inside the barrel to the top of the opposite groove. The tops of the grooves are called lands," he recited.

"Very good."

"There are three main parts in every rifle: the action, the stock and the barrel. The action is the heart of the rifle. The stock and barrel are attached to the action. This little baby's action is a semiautomatic. In other words the action does most of the work by itself. It will reload by itself, but the trigger must be pressed to fire each shot."

Tess smiled. "You have been doing your homework. Give me the highlights of what you've learned so far."

"There are three important rules. First, treat every gun as if it were loaded. Never take another's word that a gun is unloaded. Second, always be sure of the target and what is beyond it. Never shoot at anything except what you want to hit. Third, never point the muzzle at anyone, including yourself. Loaded or not."

"You learned that one by trial and error, didn't you?"

"Be nice, Tess."

"I'd be remiss if I didn't add that when you're carrying a gun you should always make sure the safety is on, that your finger is outside the trigger guard and that the firearm is kept unloaded until you begin to stalk game."

"I've got it."

She scooped up the ammunition and loaded the .22, then demonstrated the proper way to hold and sight it. When she squeezed the trigger six times in rapid succession, all of the bullets hit the bull's-eye on the paper target. She passed him the gun. "We won't spend a lot of time today on ballistics and mechanics. Just try hitting the target."

He reloaded and placed the recoil pad against his shoulder. He took aim, lining up the front bead in the notch of the rear sight. Just like the books said it would be, the target sat on top of the bead, like a pumpkin on a fence post. When he tried to fire, nothing happened.

"Don't forget to release the safety," she reminded.

He felt for the lever, found it, then disengaged it. The bull's-eye was still in place above his sights, so he pulled the trigger, steadying himself against the impact. He hit the paper, but missed the circles surrounding the center.

"Keep your aim." Tess stepped up close behind him. "Just place your fingers over mine and I'll show you what to do. When you jerk the trigger, the sights move."

Her breath tickled his neck as she spoke, and Jack stiffened involuntarily.

"Relax," she crooned into his ear. "You're much too rigid."

She didn't know the half of it, he thought wickedly. He flexed his shoulders and felt her breasts nudging him.

"Like this?" he asked innocently.

"Yes," she breathed, feeling her body's mutinous reaction to him. She took a deep breath and tried to keep her mind on the task at hand.

"Keep the target in your sights and put a slow, steady pressure on the trigger until the gun fires."

Slow and steady pressure? Was that what it would take to get her attention? he wondered.

The gun fired, and the bullet missed the target completely.

"Let's try again, Jack. First we'll steady your position." As much as she hated to do it, Tess stepped closer and wrapped her other arm around his waist. "You're breathing too hard, try to control that."

She had to be kidding! They were nestled together like two spoons, and he could feel the tips of her breasts against his back. Their hips and thighs were as close as two pairs of jeans would allow. And she wanted him to control his breathing? The woman definitely had a cruel streak.

"Got a good solid aim?" she asked in his ear.

"Yeah," he sighed. The target, Jack, he reminded himself, the target. He tried again. "Yeah."

"Take a full breath when you start squeezing the trigger. Like so."

Her breasts rose up against his shoulder blades and it was all he could do to keep from throwing down the rifle and taking her into his arms.

"Let out half the air and hold the rest until we shoot."

He tried to obey but he was mighty uncomfortable, and when the gun fired he missed again.

"Don't strain. If you hold your breath too long, your pulse hammers. That's what caused your sights to move away from the target."

"I don't think that's the problem," he said with a groan.

Tess knew she should move away from him and she did. Fast. "Why don't you try it on your own this time?"

"I've always preferred a partner for contact sports," he teased.

He was baiting her, and she wasn't about to let him get away with it. "Target practice, Jack."

He smiled, took aim and shot the bull's-eye. As with archery, it seemed that once he got the hang of it, accuracy followed. He wasn't sure who was surprised more, he or Tess, when he continued to plug the center of the target. He tried one rifle after another, with similar success.

He finally graduated to the .300 Winchester Magnum. It kicked like a mule, and Jack was sure his shoulder was broken after the first shot, but he managed to hide his pain because he didn't think he'd get much sympathy from Tess. A gunshot wound in the thigh certainly hadn't earned him any special treatment.

"Very good, Jack." She pounded him on the back like an old hunting buddy. "You really have a knack for this. You may live up to your reputation yet."

Caught off guard by her enthusiasm, he turned and took her into his arms. Wordlessly their lips met as he drew her closer to his urgent body.

Tess didn't trust her legs to hold her weight, and her arms encircled his neck. There was a welcoming hunger in the way their mouths came together. She returned his masterful kiss with fervor and felt his vitality seep into her body.

Jack knew the exact moment when Tess's newly kindled passions flared, and his own eagerness grew. But he knew she wouldn't forgive him if he allowed things to go any further at this point. He drew away from her, slowly.

"I know that wasn't supposed to happen," he said.

Alarmed by the need he aroused in her, Tess backed away. "I understand. You were just excited about your accomplishments and—"

"I'm excited all right. But not by accomplishments, Tess."

"—we'll just pretend it didn't happen."

"I've never been that good at pretending," he told her. "We want each other. We can't ignore that. It would be like ignoring a cyclone or an earthquake—impossible."

The look in his brown eyes made her hand shake as she handed him his rifle. So far, she'd been unable to resist the temptation of his kisses, the seductive effect of his caress. She'd teach him the art of ignoring. No matter what she had told him, something *was* happening, and she wasn't fighting it hard enough.

"Come on," she said briskly. "Let's go out to the meadow and shoot some game."

Once afield, Tess was all business. "Hunters use four basic positions."

"Only four positions?" He couldn't resist teasing her, she was always so serious about everything.

She ignored his suggestive tone. "Prone, sitting, kneeling and standing. The steadiest is prone—"

"That's my personal favorite."

"Shut up, Jack, and get on the ground."

He complied, then grinned up at her. "I thought you'd never ask."

She frowned down at him. "If you've been studying, you should know how to do this."

"But as in all things, it's practice that makes perfect," he said lightly. "How's this?"

"Fine . . . let your elbow and forearm support the rifle, don't try to hold it up by muscle power alone. If you don't get the position right, you'll be too uncomfortable to concentrate on your target."

"I'm concentrating already," he insisted.

"No, you aren't. And you're too tense. The secret is to relax your muscles." She hoped her scowl would put an end to further levity. "Do you have your quarry in the sights?" she challenged, knowing full well that he was watching her intently.

"I sure do."

She tipped his hunting cap over his eyes in frustration. "If you don't want to cooperate we can stop now and save ourselves a lot of time and trouble."

"Okay, okay." Jack righted his cap and peered down the rifle barrel. He was amazed to actually find a 'quarry' in his gun sight. "There's a deer out there," he yelped.

"Shh," Tess admonished. "See if you can hit it. Just draw a bead and squeeze the trigger like I taught you."

He grimaced. He didn't want to kill any of Bambi's unsuspecting relatives. The deer didn't appear to be looking for trouble as it browsed in the high grass of the meadow. It wasn't armed and dangerous. It was an innocent bystander.

He had read about buck fever, a state of excitement over an impending kill. But what he felt wasn't excitement, it was revulsion at destroying a harmless living creature. Reluctant to admit what Tess was sure to perceive as weakness, he made a decision, jerked on the trigger and deliberately missed.

But the animal just stood there, rooted to the spot. Was it deaf, or just terribly trusting? Or had he accidently shot it and the poor thing just hadn't realized it was dead yet? He was tempted to stand up and shoo it away for its own protection.

Tess didn't let up. "Try again, Jack, and squeeze slowly this time."

"No." He flicked the safety into place and scrambled to his feet.

"Why not?"

"Laugh if you want to but I refuse to shoot a defenseless animal. It's unnecessary. You told me good hunters kill only what they can eat, and I can't eat a whole deer. Maybe I could eat a squirrel,'' he rambled, ''but not a whole deer.''

Tess laughed. ''That is not a live animal, Jack. It's a deer hide and some sawdust over a wooden frame. I hate to inform you but the venison has long since been consumed in stew and meat loaf. It's a target, placed there for your benefit, to give you the feel of the sport. It's against the law to shoot deer at this time of year.''

''I knew that,'' he said defensively.

''If you had been paying attention to something besides monkey business, you would have noticed it was a target.''

She was right. He'd spotted plenty of deer on their hikes in the forest, and on closer inspection the bulky model didn't resemble those graceful animals at all. ''I wasn't very alert, was I?'' he asked sheepishly.

''Not very,'' she confirmed. ''But this points up a serious problem.''

''What kind of problem?''

''Won't you be expected to do real hunting on your show? How will you handle that?''

''I don't know, but I've about decided that I'm not cut out for blood sports. Since I've been here, I've been toying with the idea of changing the focus of the program. I don't know if the producers will go for it, but I'd like to see it move away from hunting and feature more spots about conservation, about animals and their habitats.''

''That's a wonderful idea.''

''I think the programs should be expanded for a wider audience. Hunters aren't the only people who enjoy the outdoors.''

"That's true. You could do more on hiking and backpacking. A lot of families enjoy camping vacations, and you could provide a helpful service by rating campgrounds."

"Like restaurant critics rate eating establishments. Yeah." Jack's eyes widened as he considered her idea. "We could keep the fishing spots and do more with kids. Maybe even sponsor an annual tournament for fisherman under twelve."

"You've given this some thought," she observed.

"I wouldn't have without your influence. I meant it when I said you'd given me a lot."

She looked uncomfortable and picked up the ammunition case. "Let's go back to the lodge and see if we can scare you up a squirrel for your lunch."

He fell in beside her as they walked through the sweet grass of the upland meadows. Above them the majestic mountain peaks held up the wide blue awning of sky. On the slopes the aspens were starting to turn, their dazzling golden leaves rivaling the sun in brilliance.

"Couldn't we order a pizza?" Jack asked wistfully as he matched Tess's long stride. "I miss pizza."

She walked backward so she could face him. "We're a little out of delivery range of the nearest pizzeria," she said with a laugh.

"They could put it in a cab. Can't you imagine a jumbo supreme with a thick New York crust, loaded with sausage and pepperoni and three different cheeses, wending its way up the mountain in a taxi..."

She swatted at him playfully. "Shut up, you're making my mouth water."

"Mushrooms and peppers and onions," he taunted in a singsong voice.

"I told you to shut up." Tess laughed and skipped on ahead of him.

"Someday, can I buy you a pizza?" he asked. "In a real Italian restaurant? With tables and chairs? And candles? And romantic music?"

"Maybe," she allowed, daring to hope they had such a date in their future.

He grinned. "Good. Because somewhere out there, Tess McIver, is a big gooey cheesy pizza with your name on it."

Jack wouldn't let up about the pizza and kept talking about driving into Vail. Tess didn't think it wise to allow their relationship to shift to purely social level, but Jack insisted that he wouldn't think of it as a real date if she didn't want him to.

He said he was only interested in the food, but she suspected that he needed to be around other people, even strangers. Jack wasn't used to solitude. When the subject came up again the next day, she suggested he go on without her, but he refused.

Bitterroot was on his side.

"Just go, Tessie," her father told her. "You might accidentally have some fun."

"Jack's a client, Pop. You know I have a policy about fraternizing with clients."

A deep flush crept over the old man's face. "Nobody said nothin' about fraternizin'. You're just going out to eat."

Tess smiled and went upstairs to change for her 'date.' When she came down a few minutes later, Bitterroot frowned. "That what you're wearin'?"

She looked down at the sweater and jeans. They looked fine to her. "Yes, why?"

"Cain't you wear a dress or somethin'?"

She'd almost worn a dress, but had changed her mind at the last minute. "I didn't want Jack to think I'd primped for him," she admitted.

"Don't worry, he won't."

Tess wavered. She didn't want to look like she didn't care, either. "Maybe I should wear a dress. I'll run back up and change."

Jack was waiting for her when she came down. He was dressed in a pair of gray slacks and wore a black turtleneck shirt under a gray jacket. He looked casual but sophisticated, and Tess was glad she'd changed. She'd bought the dress on impulse at a little specialty shop in Vail. Normally she didn't think much about clothes, but the gold gauze peasant dress with its delicate embroidery had caught her eye. She had few occasions to wear such an outfit and had almost returned it. Now, as she saw the admiring look in Jack's eyes, she was glad she hadn't.

Jack watched appreciatively as Tess came down the stairs. She was beautiful, but he could tell she was uncomfortable. Without the layers of thick, mannish clothes she usually wore, her figure was slender and supple. The airy fabric of her dress clung to her curves and drifted around her long, sleek legs. The metallic embroidery sparkled in the light and picked up the highlights in her hair. Tonight she wore it long and loose around her shoulders, as untamed as her spirit.

She seemed ill at ease, and he knew she had no idea how breathtaking she was, how utterly, naturally beautiful. "You look lovely, Tess," he told her.

"Am I overdressed do you think?" she asked hesitantly.

"Not at all." He extended his arm and she placed her hand on it, all the time feeling skittish and giddy. She glanced at Bitterroot as if looking for a last-minute reprieve, but her father only smiled and told them to have a good time.

On the way to town, Jack told Tess that tonight they were not allowed to discuss business. She was about to point out that business was the only thing they had in common, but he started talking about his family, and she didn't get the chance.

He told her about the tough working-class Chicago neighborhood where he'd grown up and how he'd saved for his first bike so that he could get a paper route to help out the family. He talked about summers spent working in a corner grocery store.

His parents still lived in the house where he'd grown up. When his father retired from the furniture factory and his mother from her job as a cafeteria worker in an elementary school, they'd found a rather lucrative hobby—building dollhouses.

Each one was unique. Roy Hunter designed and built them, and Vera Hunter decorated them with wallpaper samples and handmade miniatures. They'd started creating the tiny houses to keep busy, but the owner of a trendy toy store had seen one on display in a local library and offered to sell them in her shop. Demand was so high now that the Hunters had a waiting list for orders.

Jack's background surprised Tess. She had assumed his life had always been one of privilege. They had more in common, it seemed, than she'd first suspected.

"Do you have any brothers or sisters?" she asked.

"I have two sisters. The older one, Karen, is married and has a little boy. They live in Chicago. My younger sister, Ginny, just graduated from UCLA and is working for a casting agency in Los Angeles."

"I always wished I'd had siblings," Tess said. "But my mother had Hodgkin's disease. She died when I was fourteen."

"I'm sorry."

"It's all right. I missed her for a long time, but I keep her in here now." She placed her hand over her heart.

Jack sensed that Tess preferred not to talk about her loss and changed the subject. He told her funny stories about high school and how he'd gone to Dartmouth on a journalism scholarship. He'd met his wife there and they'd married soon after graduation. Like all young people in love, they'd expected to live happily ever after. They hadn't and called it quits four years later.

When they got to Vail, Tess directed Jack to an Italian restaurant that would live up to all his expectations. It had candles on the tables and mood music on the jukebox. They continued talking after ordering the biggest, cheesiest pizza on the menu.

"It's your turn," he told her. "Tell me about yourself."

"There isn't much to tell. I've lived in Big Bear all my life, I've never traveled, never been to college, never done anything that could be termed even remotely exciting." Until she said it, Tess hadn't realized how uneventful her life had been.

"Have you ever been in love?"

"No," she answered quickly before looking away. "I thought I was once, but I was wrong."

Jack wanted to urge her to talk about Greg Dexter. Not only to satisfy his own curiosity, but because he felt she needed to share her feelings with someone. She seemed to have no confidants except her father, and Jack badly wanted to be the one she could trust. But Tess didn't volunteer any more information, and he knew not to pry.

Over dinner they discovered a mutual love of reading and discussed books they'd enjoyed. When he tried to steer the conversation to more personal matters, Tess balked. She'd talk about her love for the wilderness, her love for books, her love for her life-style. But she wouldn't talk about love.

They lingered over espresso until Jack excused himself. Tess assumed he was going to the men's room, but on her way back from the ladies' she saw him talking on a pay phone in the corner. He was so absorbed in the conversation that he didn't notice her, and she wondered who he was talking to.

It stood to reason there were women in Jack's life, but it pained Tess to realize that he'd had to speak to one of them after an evening with her. No doubt, he

found her company totally lacking in the sophistica-
tion department and had to remind himself that more
interesting companions awaited him back in Denver.
He had free use of the phone at the lodge, but obviously this call was too personal to be overheard. Like
a fool, she'd been having such a good time that she
hadn't realized he wasn't.

Tess lost some of her earlier buoyancy. So what if
this evening had been the highlight of her whole summer? It meant nothing more to Jack Hunter than a
pizza and a change of scenery. She'd mistaken his attention for interest in her, and that had been a big
mistake. In fact, coming here with him at all had been
a mistake.

Jack returned and said nothing about the phone call
he'd made, further proof that it was none of her business. He tried to pick up where he'd left off, but Tess
didn't have the heart for more small talk. He suggested they make a real night of it and take in a late
movie, but she begged off. She was tired and they had
an early call in the morning.

He sensed a change in her, but didn't understand
what had caused it. He tried to engage her interest on
the drive home, but she was distant and quiet. What
had he done wrong? Had he said something to offend
her? Since she wasn't the type to talk about her feelings, he'd probably never know.

Chapter Eight

Jack never did find out what was bothering Tess and had no luck getting close to her as his training continued, without incident, for the rest of the week. Their twelve-hour training sessions presented little opportunity to think of anything but business. As he polished his gun-handling skills, she made sure he had experience with a variety of firearms, including the shotguns used in trap and skeet shooting.

She drilled him relentlessly on mechanics and ballistics, and quizzed him on hunting ethics and laws, both written and unwritten. She taught how to clean and care for weapons and to take responsibility for himself and the resources.

Bitterroot belonged to a black-powder organization that met regularly to re-create the history of the trappers and mountain men. He introduced Jack to the intricacies of muzzle-loading rifles and taught him to shoot some of the original flintlocks and caplocks in his collection.

At the archery range, Jack practiced with various bows until he could consistently hit the bull's-eye with all of them. He even learned to throw a tomahawk with some precision.

He learned the secrets of angling for bass, pike and rainbow trout and regularly provided fish for their supper. His injured leg was almost healed, and they continued hiking to build up his endurance for an extended trip into the wilderness.

Jack's head was so full of information that he feared he could never contain it all. He had no illusions that he was an outdoors expert, but by the end of the second week of his intensive training he was confident that he could learn enough to hold his own in any crowd of sportsmen.

His confidence increased as he gained practical experience to complement his book knowledge. The second half of his stay would be spent fine-tuning his skills.

He'd called Norton Greene to report his progress and had mentioned his ideas for changing the show. His old friend was enthusiastic; it seemed he'd had similar notions himself.

He didn't like to think about leaving Big Bear, and his conversation with Norton reminded him that his time with Tess was running out. On the rare occasions that he managed to break through her cool reserve, she was quick to replace the barriers that kept them apart. He knew her reluctance to get involved with him stemmed from her unhappy experience with another man, but she'd made it clear that her past was not open for discussion.

One day when she went to town for supplies, Jack approached Bitterroot. He didn't feel right going behind Tess's back, but he knew that until he understood her past better, he had no way of knowing how to get through to her.

The old man was sitting on the porch, working over a block of wood with a carving knife. He looked up and nodded when Jack joined him.

"What are you carving?" Bitterroot's gnarled hands had an easy grace that came only from years of practice, and Jack watched him in fascination.

"Ah, I like to fiddle around with a little whittlin' when I get the chance. This here piece is gonna be a bear cub if I do it right."

Jack had noticed the beautiful wood carvings of woodland creatures that decorated the lodge, but he'd never suspected they might be Bitterroot's. No primitive whittlings, the tiny pieces were painstakingly executed in realistic detail by a master craftsman. When he commented on them, the old man made light of his ability.

"You're very talented," he insisted. "That baby raccoon on the mantel looks like it could scamper off at any moment. You're hiding your light under a bushel as my mother would say. You should sell them."

Bitterroot scoffed. "Who to?"

"There's a number of galleries in Denver that would be interested. They specialize in work by local artisans."

"I ain't no artisan."

Jack smiled with pleasure as he watched the little wooden bear take shape under the knife. "You're an artist, Bitterroot, and you don't even know it."

"You reckon folks would really want to buy these?" he asked curiously.

"I'm sure of it. You not only capture the likeness of the animals, but their spirit as well. I've seen pieces not nearly as good as yours sell for hundreds of dollars."

Bitterroot's eyes widened. "No foolin'?"

"I know some people who would jump at the chance to take your work on consignment. I'd be happy to take back some pieces to show them."

He pondered that suggestion. "You really think anybody'd buy 'em?"

"I'm sure of it. In fact, I want to be your first customer. I'd like to send that raccoon to my mother for her birthday. That is, if it's for sale."

"If you want it, it's yours."

"You set the price."

Bitterroot scratched his stubbly chin. "Lordy, I wouldn't have no idea how much somethin' like that would be worth to anyone 'cept myself."

"Would three hundred and fifty be enough?" Jack ventured.

"Dollars!" he spluttered. "You talkin' U.S. currency, boy?"

"I told you, it's art. And art carries a pretty price tag." Jack could almost see the wheels turning in Bitterroot's mind.

"Lordy, if I could sell enough of them critters, I could fix this place up."

"I have no doubt you will." Jack was not flattering the old man. He knew there was a market for the appealing sculptures. It wouldn't be difficult to tap it.

They talked at length about the possibilities until Jack brought up the subject that had disturbed him so long.

"Bitterroot, what did Greg Dexter do to Tess?" he asked bluntly.

The old man showed little surprise at the abrupt change of subject. "I was wonderin' when you'd get around to askin'."

"I'd hoped Tess would talk to me, but that doesn't seem likely. I hate to pry into her personal affairs, but I need to know."

"I reckon you do. She'll prob'ly accuse me of talkin' out of school, but it ain't right for her to keep it bottled up, festerin' inside her."

"Who was he?" Jack had no hold over Tess, yet it disturbed him to think of her with another man. Especially one who had hurt her.

"Oh, he was a smooth-talkin' con man. Only we didn't know that at the time. Three years ago he came up here from Denver for a week's fishin' and landed Tess's heart instead. I guess you'd call it one of them whirlwind courtships, but he plumb turned her head."

"Tess?" Jack asked incredulously. "Clearheaded, down-to-earth Tess? That's a blow to my ego. I've been knocking myself out trying to get her attention."

"She ain't exactly the same girl she was back then." Bitterroot's voice was tinged with bitterness toward the man who had duped his daughter.

It was a case of fool me once, Jack thought.

Bitterroot seemed to read his mind. "To Tess's credit, I gotta say he fooled me, too. He claimed he loved her, and she was ready to be loved. Her mama died when she was fourteen, an age when a girl needs her mother most. She kinda turned into herself after that.

"When she finished high school, I tried to get her to go off to college, to broaden her horizons, like. She's plenty smart enough, but she ain't never wanted to leave Big Bear. Maybe I shoulda made her go. That's what a mama grizzly does when it's time for her young ones to learn to fend for themselves. Just flat runs 'em up a tree and leaves 'em."

"You said Dexter was a con man?" Jack prompted.

"I'm gettin' to that part." Bitterroot's knife flashed as he carved the bear's hindquarters. "Tess was born here and grew up around men, but she's always been innocent of their ways. I never had much use for the world, and I reckon I protected her too much. Anyway, Dexter shows up claiming to be some hotshot businessman, and before you know it, Tess was in love. He came back several times, courtin' her, bringin' her presents and stealin' her trust.

"Then one trip he started talkin' about how he was gettin' tired of city life. Of how he was lookin' for a good investment and a quiet place to live. He said if we mortgaged the lodge and combined the proceeds with his investment capital, we could turn Big Bear into the most successful lodge in the Rockies."

"I suppose that would appeal to anyone," Jack commented.

"I wasn't so keen on the idea. My grandpappy built this place and it never had a lien agin it, but he and Tess was talkin' marriage and she wanted to do it."

Jack felt a sick sense of dread. He knew what was coming, but prompted Bitterroot anyway. "Go on."

"The long and the short of it is we mortgaged Big Bear to the hilt, and Greg Dexter tucked our money into his fancy briefcase and left for Denver to make all the arrangements for renovations."

"And never came back," Jack guessed.

"That's right. Tess got mighty worried when she didn't hear from him like he promised. She phoned his home but the number had been disconnected. She called the highfalutin firm where he claimed to work, but they never heard of him. I'll tell you, it was one heartsick gal who finally called the police."

"What did they do?"

"There wasn't nothin' they could do. But they told her Greg Dexter was only one of his aliases and that he was a professional con man who preyed on lonely women. They put our name on some list or other, but we never heard no more about it. I reckon he's still out there, doin' what he does best—ruinin' lives."

Jack had heard of such criminals, men who used love as a weapon to rob their victims of something more valuable than money—their self-esteem. Not only had Tess been disillusioned about men and love, she'd lost faith in herself and her ability to judge. It was no wonder she worked so hard to stay aloof.

Bitterroot wasn't finished. "I tried to tell Tessie it weren't her fault. That he'd suckered me, too. But she was bitter to the bone. Said she should have known a man as sophisticated as Greg Dexter couldn't possibly be interested in a backwoods girl like her. She turned hard, she did. And swore she'd never be taken in by a phony again.''

"Then along came Hunter,'' Jack said, then groaned. Despite his necessary deception on the show, he'd never thought of himself as a phony. He'd always wanted the experience he needed to be authentic and had never been comfortable pretending to be something he wasn't. But in light of what he'd just heard, he understood why Tess considered him a phony and why she refused to allow him get close to her.

"Maybe now you can understand why she's so unwillin' to trust you, boy.''

"But that was three years ago. Why is she still beating up on herself? And on me?''

Bitterroot sighed. "Dexter left us in a world of hurt, financially speakin'. We dang near lost the lodge that first year, but we managed to hang on by the skin of our teeth. It's been hard on Tess, feelin' like it was her fault and all. Bein' reminded every day of a mistake that shoulda been forgiven and forgotten a long time ago. That's why she works so hard and goes without things a woman like her ought to have. It ain't right, but she's so danged stubborn!''

Jack patted the old man's shoulder. "The mortgage still isn't paid off?'' he asked gently.

Bitterroot snorted. "Not by a long shot. We got two more years to pay on it. And in the meantime, the place is fallin' in on our heads 'cause we ain't got the money for repairs.'' He whacked his ankle cast in derision before he remembered he was talking to an outsider. "'Course, we'll survive. McIvers always do."

Jack was silent for a few moments, absorbing the implications of the story he'd just heard. Poor Tess. She'd been a young girl ripe for her first love. And the man had used it against her. He'd left her without a second thought for what his greed and callousness would do to her life.

Jack knew how much Big Bear meant to her, how long it had been in her family. If it were lost to an uncaring bank, she would never be able to live with the guilt. He couldn't let that happen.

"Look, Bitterroot. I know you McIvers have survived hostile Indian attacks and blizzards and grizzly bears over the past hundred years. But have you ever tangled with the modern institution of banking?"

"None except the young weasel who calls up and reads us the riot act when we're late with the payment."

"Maybe I can help."

"Nah, it ain't your problem."

"I have some money—"

Bitterroot held up his hand. "Whoa there! I ain't borrowin' no more money. Especially from a friend. No, Jack, you just stop thinkin' like that. Why, Tess would hit the ceilin' if you offered to loan us money."

"Not loan. Invest. As bad as Dexter's character was, he *did* have a good idea. I'm willing to assume your mortgage and provide capital for repairs. With necessary improvements, the lodge could attract more guests and pay me back in no time."

Bitterroot looked skeptical. "I don't know. What would you get out of all this?"

"Return on my investment and the satisfaction of helping my friends out of a tight spot. I owe you that much, Bitterroot. You and Tess have given me so much."

"Well, it sounds good to me, but I can tell you right now, Tess won't go for it."

Jack sighed. No, she wouldn't. She'd heard it all before, and she wasn't sure yet if he could be trusted. But since she was always telling him that actions spoke louder than words, he'd just have to show her. He gave Bitterroot a companionable pat on the shoulder. "You leave Tess to me."

A car engine backfired and the two men looked up to see Maddie's old bug coughing and sputtering its way up the road. It died in the yard and she hopped out, waving a bundle.

"Yoo-hoo!" she trilled. "I come bearing goodies."

"Oh, lordy," Bitterroot groaned. "I wish I could leave that one to you, too." With a desperate look, he got up and hurried down the steps.

Maddie brightened when she saw the old man limping toward her, but her face fell when he jumped on his three-wheeler and turned the vehicle down the driveway.

"Bitterroot," she called after him. "I made you a batch of my special molasses cookies."

"Past time for the mailman," he yelled back as though that would explain his haste.

Maddie shrugged and turned to Jack. "I hope you like molasses cookies, young man."

"I sure do."

Bitterroot was gone a long time and Jack suspected that fetching the mail wasn't his real reason for disappearing so suddenly. Both the McIvers, it seemed, were a little gun-shy when it came to romance. He sat on the porch eating cookies and tried to find out more about Maddie and her motives.

He soon learned that she'd never been married, that she lived in Vail with her elderly mother and was on vacation from her job as the head of housekeeping for a major motel there. She'd put in thirty years and would be retiring in a few months, at which time she hoped to turn her avocation into a vocation for her sunset years.

"And what might that be?" Jack asked suspiciously. He still thought the flighty old woman wasn't exactly telling him the whole story. She was lonely and she seemed taken with Bitterroot, but she wasn't pursuing the acquaintance just so she'd have an excuse to bake molasses cookies.

"Why, I've always harbored a secret ambition to write," she confessed. "I've composed reams of poetry and short stories, but so far I've been unable to interest a publisher in my work."

"I've always wanted to write novels myself," he confided. Prodding for more information, he asked, "Have you ever considered newspaper reporting?"

Maddie looked alarmed. "Me? A reporter? I don't have the credentials for a *real* reporting job," she said uneasily.

Jack was sure she was holding back information, and was about to ask her what she meant, when Tess's Jeep roared into the yard and slammed to a halt. Bitterroot was right behind her on his three-wheeler. It was a very disgruntled Tess who started toward the lodge with a double armload of grocery sacks.

Jack jumped up to help her, but she pushed past him. "I don't need you, I can manage quite nicely on my own, thank you. I managed before you came here and I will manage again when you leave." She scarcely looked in Maddie's direction.

Bitterroot hobbled in behind her with another bag of supplies, and Jack asked, "What happened to make Tess so angry?"

"Why don't you ask her?" He nodded at Maddie.

"Maddie?" Jack asked.

"Oh, dear," the woman cried and wrung her hands. "I had hoped I'd gotten here in time. Oh dear."

"In time for what?" Jack demanded.

Tess came out and the screen door banged behind her. She thrust a tabloid paper into his face.

"Why don't you read all about it?" she asked sarcastically.

"Oh, dear!" Maddie wailed.

"How could you?" Tess demanded of the woman. "I thought you were our friend."

Jack unfolded the latest issue of the *StarGazer Gazette* and saw his face staring back at him. He quickly flipped to the inside and shuffled past stories about a woman who claimed to be the reincarnation of Mary Todd Lincoln and a mynah bird that could predict earthquakes. Plastered all over the center spread he found photos of him and Tess fishing, kissing and clenching.

The headline screamed; Jack Hunter Secretly Married And Honeymooning At Secluded Lake. The pictures could only have been snapped from the cover of lakeside bushes, and Jack recalled the noise he had attributed to a bear.

He turned the paper in his hands and viewed the photos from a different angle. They weren't professional quality, but Maddie had certainly captured the spirit of the moment.

"Oh, boy," he muttered.

"Is that all you have to say?" Tess demanded.

"Do you think I did this?" he asked incredulously.

"No. I think she did." Tess turned to Maddie, her hands clamped firmly on her hips. "What I don't know is why."

The old woman sobbed her confession. "Yes, yes, yes. I sent in the story and the photographs."

"Why?" Tess repeated.

"I recognized Jack when you two were leaving the hospital. I hang out there on weekends hoping to get a scoop on some movie star or other. Vail's full of them, you know."

"That explains nothing, Maddie," Jack intoned. "Just tell us everything."

"Oh, dear," Maddie wailed again. "Well, I checked with my friend at the admitting desk, and when she showed me his admission papers, I thought there'd been a mistake."

Jack sighed. "But like a good reporter you persisted."

"I know Jack Hunter when I see him, and since I hadn't heard anything about your marriage, I thought you were using an alias to keep it quiet. That's why I came nosing around here. Because I dared to hope I had my very first exclusive. I called the *StarGazer* office in Denver, and the editor wanted the story. I couldn't believe it. It was my big break."

"Oh, boy," Jack repeated.

Bitterroot laughed so hard he had to sit down before his bum ankle gave out on him.

"Will you stop saying that?" Tess snapped at Jack. "And you Pop, stop laughing. This is not funny. Didn't anybody famous do anything newsworthy this week? Get a divorce, have a face-lift, check into a rehab center?"

A teary-eyed Maddie tried to smile. "I never meant any harm, especially once I got to know all of you." She gazed fondly at Bitterroot, then turned to Jack. "I know you wanted to protect your privacy, but the truth has to come out sooner or later. And I thought, better me than someone else."

Bitterroot laughed harder.

"But the truth didn't come out at all. And when it does, we're all going to look like a bunch of fools," Tess said with a flash of temper.

"I don't understand," Maddie said.

"No, I guess you don't. Pop! Stop that laughing right now."

Bitterroot clapped his hand over his mouth in an effort to do so, but he caught Jack's eye and the two men dissolved in gales of laughter.

"This is *not* funny!" Tess yelled.

Maddie wrung her hands some more. "Don't be mad at me, Tess dear. I didn't do it with malicious intent. I just wanted the world to share in your happiness. Please say you forgive me. Please?" she pleaded.

"Oh, all right, I forgive you. But how are we going to explain this?"

"One need never explain the truth," Maddie placated.

"The truth?" Tess asked. "Are you really ready for that, Maddie? Seeing as you're a member of the esteemed press, I'll tell you, but it's off the record. Jack and I are not married at all."

Maddie gasped. "You're not?"

Tess shook her head. "Never have been—never will be."

"Oh, dear." The old woman's eyes widened until her untidy eyebrows disappeared under her wig. "Not married? Oh, dear."

"Oh dear, is right." Tess scanned the paper and read aloud, " 'The newlyweds are reportedly spending their honeymoon at a remote Colorado lodge.' At least they didn't print the name and location."

"I was very specific about that," Maddie said self-righteously. "I didn't want you two to be disturbed, so I claimed I was protecting my sources. The editor said he called round trying to verify the story and was unable to corroborate anything. But he couldn't say no to the pictures."

"He must have been the one who called here the other day," Bitterroot put in.

"I don't know why you're so angry, Tess," Jack said. "This rag isn't exactly famous for hard-hitting journalism. Their big stories usually involve sightings of aliens, Bigfoot or Elvis. We're lucky to even make it into print.''

''You call this lucky?'' Tess flicked the pictures with her hand. ''At least they didn't print the real reason you're here.''

''What is the real reason?'' Maddie brightened at the prospect of a new and juicier story.

''Never mind that,'' Tess instructed. ''What will your producers think when they read this?''

''They'll probably be relieved that the real reason for me being here didn't leak out.''

''What is the real reason?'' Maddie asked again.

Tess ignored her. ''The paper will just have to print a retraction.''

''Papers like this don't print retractions,'' Jack pointed out.

Maddie moaned. ''There goes my career down the dumper.''

Bitterroot patted her consolingly on the back.

''Career? Maddie, this was your first story,'' Jack reminded her.

''That's what I mean,'' she cried. ''It's dead before it even lived.''

Jack filled Tess and Bitterroot in on Maddie's journalistic ambitions. When he was finished, he said brightly, ''No one has to lose face here. There's a simple solution to the problem.''

Maddie and Bitterroot turned to him expectantly.

Tess looked skeptical. ''And what might that be?''

''We could really get married.''

''Oh, right,'' she hooted. ''Be serious, Jack.''

"I'm perfectly serious," he confirmed.

"Maybe you're willing to sacrifice yourself to protect Maddie's budding career as a tabloid tattler, but I'm certainly not."

"Tess—" Jack began.

She raced up the stairs, and a slamming door was her only reply. He took the stairs two a time behind her and pounded for her to open up and talk to him.

"I don't want to talk about this," she yelled.

"Oh, dear," Maddie wailed. "I've botched things horribly, haven't I?"

Bitterroot scratched his chin and seemed to consider the situation. "The way I see it, there's nothin' like a frog in the punch bowl to stir things up."

Chapter Nine

Jack's offhanded proposal hurt Tess more than she cared to admit, and she retreated further into herself. She refused to talk to him about anything personal, and even threatened to end his training prematurely if he didn't drop the matter and get back to work. When he obeyed, she suffered mixed feelings that kept her awake at night and made every hour she spent with him exquisite torture.

Because so much was unresolved between them, she dreaded the upcoming wilderness hike and the forced togetherness it would impose on them. She considered canceling the trip, but pride won out and she continued with the planned excursion as though nothing had changed. Jack made several earnest attempts to speak privately with her, but she wasn't accustomed to discussing her feelings, and he finally gave up trying.

He made several trips into Vail, but did not ask her to join him. No doubt he was secretly relieved when she hadn't taken him seriously, and was eager to return to his real life. She didn't want to care, but the prospect of his leaving chilled her as much as a cold mountain wind. No matter how much the fact angered her, no matter how much she tried to deny it, the truth was heartbreakingly simple.

She loved Jack Hunter and there was nothing she could do about it.

Surprisingly there were no repercussions from Maddie's startling confession. Because the name of the lodge hadn't been listed in the article, no reporters called demanding interviews, and no curious fans disturbed their peace.

As Jack had predicted, the producers of his show had not taken the story seriously and had breathed a collective sigh of relief that the real reason for his sojourn had not been revealed to the public. They had received phone calls from fans of the show, but the station's representative had judiciously used the "no comment" loophole.

To everyone's surprise, Bitterroot became Maddie's staunchest defender, and Tess wondered if her father hadn't finally succumbed to the old woman's dubious charms. After much reassurance that they wouldn't hold the story against her, she had returned to Vail in apologetic tears. She said the mess she had created was enough to make her stick to poetry in the future. Maybe her epics would never be published, but at least they wouldn't hurt anyone, either.

A week later Tess and Jack embarked on the extended backpacking trip that was to serve as his final exam. They planned to climb to the summit of Mount McIver, a peak named for Tess's ancestor who had first explored the area.

That part of the wilderness was on federal lands and open to outdoor enthusiasts, but only the hardiest souls attempted the rugged climb this time of year. It was truly a wilderness; there were no Park Service campgrounds, no you-are-here signs, and very few designated trails.

The test of his knowledge had begun even before they left the lodge. With Tess's supervision, he organized their packs and food supplies. He obtained the necessary camping and fire permits, and together they went over a map of the area and marked their route to file at the nearest ranger station. She was the guide on this trip, but he was no longer a tenderfoot tagalong.

His wound was completely healed, and he was confident he could keep up whatever pace she set. He'd given up trying to discuss his feelings for her at Big Bear, but he had most definitely not given up on her. Or on them. He was scared by the speed with which his love for her had eclipsed everything he had formerly deemed important in life, but he knew better than to try and understand how it had happened. He had to concentrate all his energy on convincing her that he was sincere.

Which, given the events of the past week, would be no easy task. That's why the hiking trip was so important. Out in the wild there would be no doors to keep him out, no walls to hide behind except the ones she constructed around her heart. If he chose the moment carefully, waiting until they were far from the lodge, she'd be a captive audience.

The stubborn woman would have to listen to him then, and he meant to make her accept reality by whatever means necessary. Fate had brought them together. Who were they to deny it?

They planned to be gone four days and three nights; a lot could happen in that length of time. A lot of questions could be raised and answered, a lot of doubts laid to rest, a lot of trust restored. All alone and far from outside distractions, much could be settled at last. Jack sensed the desperation in Tess's reserve and dared to hope that she cared as much for him as he did for her.

He'd gambled everything on that hope.

Jack found his rhythm early in the hike, freeing his mind for other thoughts. He couldn't help comparing this trip to his first outing. Thinking back, he'd been a pretty poor sport. He'd complained about everything: the heavy pack, the heat, the insects. Now he hardly noticed such insignificant details. He was too busy reveling in a sky painted brilliant morning colors, vistas that went on forever.

Before, he'd felt compelled to fill the silence of the forest with the sound of his own voice. Now he treasured the companionable silence that allowed him to be part of his surroundings. He was gratified by the knowledge that when he moved through the forest, he left no sign of himself behind.

Since the first white men had come to America, their goal had been to change the land and wrest it into submission. In their zeal to possess, they cut down the trees, diverted the rivers, destroyed the animals and fouled the environment. Some things were lost forever, but Tess and Bitterroot had taught him that it wasn't too late. It was never too late.

As Jack strode across a sparkling mountain stream, he realized how grateful he was for the experience he'd had at Big Bear. There had been moments when he would have chucked the whole natural planet for a martini and a soft bed, but he hadn't. With perseverance he had learned much more than he'd ever bargained for.

But as wonderful as his newfound love of nature was, it was nothing compared to the love he felt for Tess McIver.

She hadn't given him a chance to tell her about his talk with Bitterroot or about his plans to rescue the lodge and insure himself a place in her life. Neither had he told her he loved her, for he hadn't known how. It was as hard to love Tess as it was impossible not to.

She had a proud spirit and uncommon strength. She was practical, sensible and intelligent, but what attracted Jack most was her goodness. She represented solidity and roots and a sense of belonging that Jack hadn't even known he needed until he met her.

She'd been hurt, and she had compensated by locking up her heart. He only hoped he held the key to open it. Three weeks ago he'd wanted to teach her to trust so that she could love again. Now he wanted her to love only him.

"Ready for a break?" Her clear voice interrupted his reverie.

"Only if you are." Their packs were heaviest at the outset of their trip, and they planned to cover the fewest miles per day at the beginning. After four hours of hiking they'd stopped only twice for a few minutes at a time.

"We may as well enjoy the scenery," she said.

He stepped up behind her and saw that she had stopped at the edge of a mountain overlook. The sun was bright, the sky was clear and they could see for miles in every direction. Majestic peaks rose to the north, and a distant lake shimmered in the sunlight.

"It's beautiful," he whispered reverently.

"It's one of my favorite spots up here." Tess could feel Jack's warmth, and ached for his touch. He hadn't been his usual teasing self lately, and she missed the verbal sparring that had characterized their relationship before things had grown so tense between them. He was newly serious, as though contemplating something painful.

He'd be leaving in less than a week, and she already missed him. She should curse him for bringing so much temporary happiness into her life, but she knew it wasn't only his fault. Before Jack she'd been able to pretend that she had everything she wanted, that her solitary life suited her fine.

Then he'd come along, with his winning ways and wicked charm, and shown her how wrong she'd been. He'd demonstrated how much she'd missed of life, how much she needed someone to love.

She still had her father and the lodge. At least they had Big Bear for as long as they could continue to hold on. After Greg, she'd thrown herself into work, losing herself in the wild beauty of her home. It had been enough to help her get over him. She hadn't forgotten what he'd done, but memories of him no longer had the power to hurt her.

She suffered no illusions that things would be so simple when Jack left. No amount of physical labor or worry over bankruptcy would make her forget the magic of his kisses, his funny tenderness, or the joy she felt just being in the same room with him. Why did she have to fall in love again?

"Tess?"

She felt his hand on her shoulder and gathered her wits about her. "We'd better move on. If we stop too long our muscles will tighten up."

"I was just wondering if you were going to notice that, or if I'd have to bring it up myself," she lied.

Jack watched her stride away, her long legs pumping rhythmically, her hips swaying beneath the pack she carried with ease. Like the wilderness, she was untouched and unfettered by the restrictions of society, and it would be criminally selfish to try and change either one for his convenience.

That's why their relationship had seemed so impossible at first. His life was back in Denver, hers was here in these mountains. In order to be together, one of them would have to make a sacrifice. It had seemed like a win-lose proposition.

When the solution had finally come to him, it had been amazing in its simplicity.

* * *

They made camp that night in a sheltered area near a running stream, and after a supper of tinned beef and rehydrated vegetables, spread their sleeping bags beside the tidy keyhole fire Jack built. He sat on his bedroll, unusually quiet and tense, staring at the fire.

"Is something on your mind?" Tess asked nervously.

"A lot of things."

"Would it help to talk about them?" She knew she was courting disaster, but she couldn't contain her curiosity any longer.

"Yes, but you may not like what I have to say."

Tess stiffened. "Try me."

"I asked Bitterroot about Greg Dexter—"

"You had no right," she accused.

"I think I have a right to know why you refuse to let me into your life."

"And now you know," she said sarcastically.

"I think I understand a lot of things better, yes." He stood up and walked around the fire. She tensed when he sat down beside her on her sleeping bag. "You can't go on hiding from love because of one mistake, Tess."

"What makes you such an expert on what I should or shouldn't do?" she demanded.

"I don't claim to be an expert. I'm just a highly interested party." He placed his hands on her shoulders and drew her close enough to smell the flowery fragrance of her hair. After a moment she relaxed in his arms and he pressed her head to his chest, cradling her tenderly. The need to tell her he loved her was a physical ache inside him, but it was too soon for declarations.

As headstrong as she was, she might turn around and march back to the lodge. He'd save his speech for tomorrow night's campfire. In the meantime, he would try to prove his love without words.

"Bitterroot is worried about you," he said softly. "So am I."

"I can take care of myself." Tess had allowed his caress because she was starving for his touch, but now she tried to separate from him.

He wouldn't let her. He just kept holding her. "I know you can. You are the most totally self-sufficient female I have ever met. But you don't have to be. Can't you let anyone else care about you?"

"Jack, please—"

"You can't use teaching me as an excuse anymore. I'm taught. You did a wonderful job because you respected me enough not to make things easy for me. Whether you want to admit it or not, you cared enough not to let me manipulate you into an awkward position and for that, *I* respect *you*."

She looked up at him and her eyes glimmered in the firelight. "I care a lot, Jack. More than I ever wanted to. But it would be reckless for us to give in to our desire, because nothing meaningful could come of it. Don't you understand?"

He understood only that he had to kiss her. His lips branded hers with a fire that had smoldered for three weeks, and he savored the sweet taste of her. The kiss went on and on, unhurried, because they were all alone and there would be no interruptions. The night and all its wild magic belonged to them.

He eased her down on the sleeping bag and slipped a hand beneath her flannel shirt. She moaned when he unclasped her bra and cupped her breast. He teased her nipples into hard peaks and she moved languidly against him, sighing her pleasure.

He freed her long hair from its holder and burrowed his fingers in the silky mass. He fought his growing need for her, knowing that hunger and haste could destroy forever his chances of winning her trust.

He was caught between the opposing forces of sense and sensation, and a rumbling sigh was the only sign of his inner battle. He wanted to give this woman his heart, but he knew now that she'd possessed his soul since the first moment they met.

Tess gloried in Jack's embrace and knew she was dancing on the brink. Another touch, another kiss, and she would be unable to deny him anything he asked of her.

She was tired of pretending she didn't want him. Such sham required more skill than she possessed. Even if they had no future together, they had the night. Maybe a few stolen hours of pleasure would be enough to see her through years of loneliness.

She deepened the kiss, and Jack moaned as he set her away from him. Visibly shaken, he raked a hand through his hair and let out a deep breath. "That was close," he muttered in the same thunderstruck tone of voice he would use after jumping out of the path of an oncoming bus.

The night was cool, and without his nearness to warm her, Tess shivered involuntarily.

"You'd better get in your sleeping bag," he advised as he fought for control. He busied himself banking the fire for the night and tried not to think about how perfectly she had fit in his arms.

Tess nodded and slipped into her makeshift bed. Why had he stopped? She'd felt his desire, sensed his need. Why had he called a halt to what might have been a glorious night of lovemaking? Obviously he hadn't wanted her as much as she'd wanted him. Or had he found her lacking?

"Jack?" Her voice was a tremor in the dark.

"Yes, Tess?"

"Good night." She almost invited him into her sleeping bag, but her fear of rejection and her lack of confidence in her own appeal made her change her mind.

Jack crawled inside his down bag and zipped it with a resolve he didn't feel. It would be a long time until morning. "Good night, Tess."

They rose early the next morning and both were careful not to mention the close call of the night before. As the day progressed, they spoke less and less because uphill hiking precluded all but the most perfunctory speech. They saved their breath for the climb.

The scenery was spectacular. At this elevation the aspens were in full autumn color, their bright golden leaves shimmered and quaked in the breeze. The rarefied air made breathing more difficult, but the sweet, pine-clean scent more than compensated for that slight inconvenience.

As usual Tess led the way because she knew the area and all its hazards. Today they were following a rambling old game trail that disappeared completely in places. It was narrow and rocky and littered with loose stones weathered out of the surrounding rocks. Its many twists and turns led them around immovable boulders and past sheer drops that took their breath away when they looked down to the ravines below.

"You said this was a game trail, right?" Jack called to Tess after safely maneuvering a scenic but frighteningly narrow bit of a trail. "What kind of game, mountain goats?"

"Probably."

"Mountain goats, I should have known. Has anyone ever thought of building an elevated tram up to Mount McIver?" he asked facetiously. "It would certainly save time."

"It wouldn't be quite the same. Keep climbing, Jack," she advised, "and pay attention. This part of the trail can be treacherous."

He followed in silence for a few more minutes. They would be making camp for the night soon, and his thoughts churned as he considered how best to tell Tess what was on his mind. They were miles away from the lodge now, and tonight would be the perfect time to talk to her.

"How much longer before we make camp?" he asked, no longer caring if she knew how tired he was.

"Not long."

She'd been unusually taciturn all day, and he tried again to engage her attention. Maybe levity would work. "I think that's the best thing about hiking—stopping."

Her only response was a grunt.

Forget levity. "I talked to Norton the other day. He likes the ideas we had about changing the show."

"Good."

"If we can talk the producers into going along with us, the image of the host won't be so important."

"You don't have to worry about image anymore, Jack. By the time this hike is over, you will have earned your outdoorsman badge," she called over her shoulder as she cautiously worked her way around a fallen tree.

But will I have earned your love? he wanted to ask her. Before he could say anything, she stopped and looked up, her keen eyes picking out the dark shape of a soaring eagle against the wide blue sky. "Look!"

Enrapt, Jack raised his binoculars and watched the magnificent bird swoop and glide. It's aerial maneuvers were all wild grace, its shrieking call triumphant freedom. "I've never seen anything like it," he breathed in fascinated wonder.

"Not many people ever do," she told him. "As many times as I've witnessed it, I never quite get used to the sight."

"Seeing that eagle makes the climb worthwhile," he said honestly. Then in an equally serious tone, he teased, "I'm glad my first time was with someone as experienced as you."

He was such a tease that Tess decided to ignore him for the rest of the day and started to move on, wending her way past another drop.

"Speaking of first times—" he began.

"I don't believe we were," she interrupted, her frustration apparent. "Will you stop jabbering and pay attention to the trail?"

No sooner had the last word left her mouth than Tess slipped on a pile of loose rocks. Jack saw her struggle to maintain her balance, but the heavy pack made it impossible. He ran to help her but he was too late, and she toppled over the edge of the ravine.

Although it took only a split second for disaster to strike, Tess lived the moment in slow motion. She felt the slide of rubble under the heavy sole of her boot and knew she would fall.

She tried to shift the backpack to regain her lost balance, but the weight and the momentum were already carrying her down. She braced herself for the impact but realized too late that she'd plunged off the trail and was careening down the side of the mountain.

Jack watched in helpless horror as Tess disappeared over the edge of the ravine. Freeing himself from momentary inaction, he rushed to the spot where she'd fallen, terrified at what he would find when he looked below.

Tess felt the rocks and branches tear at her as she skidded down the incline on her back and instinctively protected her face and eyes. The heavy pack absorbed most of the shock and damage. She still had full use of her limbs and assumed that none had yet been broken.

She was falling at an alarming speed and her only hope of escaping serious injury was to stop her wayward descent before she struck a boulder or deadfall.

Or the bottom of the ravine.

She grappled for a handhold but the vegetation uprooted in her hands and abraded the tender skin through her leather gloves. From above she heard Jack's frenzied voice screaming her name and prayed he would have the foresight not to follow her down in some misguided rescue attempt. She wanted to call out to him, but the world was whizzing past so quickly that she could not spare the effort.

One moment she was moving, the next she was yanked to a sudden jarring halt and her head was pounded forcefully on a rock. Fighting the white-hot pain that exploded inside her skull, she opened her eyes and saw that she had come to rest on a narrow ledge jutting out over the gorge. Far below, jagged boulders and the accumulated debris of nature made the bottom an inhospitable place for tourists.

When she tried to sit up, she found her pack snagged on an exposed tree root. Moving carefully lest she dislodge herself from her precarious perch, she slipped her arms out of the pack's straps and collapsed against it.

Jack watched as Tess jerked to a halt on the ledge below. He didn't know what had stopped her dangerous tumble, but he was overwhelmingly relieved that something had. She was so still, her face so ashen, that he thought she was unconscious. When he sighted through his binoculars he saw her eyes flutter open, and he sighed audibly as she gingerly removed her pack.

Before he could call to her, she apparently tried to find a safer position on the ledge. The movement caused part of the loose rock to crumble and sent her pack crashing down the ravine.

"Tess!" he yelled down. "Don't move. Just hold on, I'll get you out of there."

She wanted to advise him on the best possible course of action, but all the breath had been pounded out of her on the way down. She fought a wave of nausea and the blackness that threatened to engulf her. She couldn't pass out. If she did, she'd fall just as the pack had fallen. She had to concentrate every bit of energy she had left just to hold on.

She'd have to trust Jack to orchestrate her rescue.

Chapter Ten

In his panic to save Tess, Jack feared he would forget everything she had taught him. Before he could make a dangerous mistake, he took a deep breath. She had told him there were two important rules of wilderness survival. Stay calm in an emergency. Think before you act.

"Tess! Can you hear me?"

"I hear you, Jack." Her weak reply barely made it up the slope.

"Don't move."

"Don't worry, I won't." She didn't think he heard that, but her voice wasn't working right. Carefully, so as not to loosen any more of the ledge, she moved her limbs and checked for injury.

Her body was already sore from its wild tumble over rocks and pinecones and vegetation. She would no doubt bear colorful bruises for a while, but she was sure no bones were broken. Her head hurt and the nausea made her wonder if she'd suffered a concussion.

Up top, Jack uncoiled the length of rope he carried, praying it would be long enough. He tied one end around a tree using two half hitches and secured the other end to his waist. His lessons had not covered rappeling, but he couldn't worry about his novice status now. He'd just have to improvise as he went along. Holding firmly to the line, he lowered himself over the edge of the ravine.

It took him only a few heart-pounding minutes to reach her. She was shaken and a little stunned but looked as though she had escaped serious injury, and he was thankful for that.

"God, you scared me." He hugged her close, hard hit by the realization that he couldn't live without this sweet, exasperating, wonderfully precious woman of his.

"Me, too." Tess clung to him. Adrenaline had poured into her system during the fall, but now it had receded and she felt weak and trembly.

"Are you sure you're all right?"

"Yes, I'm just banged up a bit. I'll be fine." She looked down and shuddered at the frightening prospect below. "Once I get off this ledge, that is."

Before she could say more, Jack sprung into action. He removed the rope from his waist and secured it to hers.

"Now you'll be safe even if the ledge crumbles. I'm going back up. When I get to the top I'll pull you up.

All you have to do is hold on and use your feet to keep your body from swinging into the rocks.''

"I can do that." At least she could unless she passed out, which was a distinct possibility considering the way her head throbbed.

"Good." He kissed her firmly on the lips before climbing nimbly hand over hand up the dangling rope. Going up took longer than going down, but within minutes he called to her from above. "Are you ready, Tess?"

"Ready," she answered. Tess shook her head to clear it, but try as she would she could not organize her thoughts into a sensible pattern. In her present condition she could not have gotten herself to safety, and it was a relief to place herself in Jack's capable hands. It felt good not to be in charge for a change.

When the dizzying ascent was over Jack pulled her into his arms. "I'm so sorry, Tess," he whispered.

His image blurred and she fought to stay upright. "For what?"

"If I hadn't been fooling around and distracting you like I was, you never would have fallen. It's all my fault."

"That's crazy," she told him as emphatically as she could manage. "It was an accident. It could have happened to anyone. Don't blame yourself."

"Do you think you need medical attention? Can you walk?"

She considered his question for a moment before answering. "I don't think so." The world spun again and Jack caught her as she lost consciousness.

* * *

He made her comfortable and tended her injuries, but he was worried when, an hour later, she was still out cold. He had given her rudimentary first aid and prayed that was good enough. He could only hope she hadn't suffered internal injuries that were beyond his scope and ability to diagnose.

He couldn't leave her alone to go for help, and no one was likely to come along in this little-traveled area. They'd filed their plans and weren't due back at the lodge until day after tomorrow, so no one would be looking for them yet.

Jack was on his own. He busied himself making camp and hoped Tess would regain consciousness soon.

When she finally came to, Tess was surprised how long she'd been out. Day was gone, but night had not fully arrived, and the forest was quiet at this changing of the guard. The air was chilly, but she was tucked snugly into Jack's sleeping bag close to a crackling fire complete with bubbling cook pot.

He was crouched beside it, stirring the contents of the pot. His back was to her, and even in her condition she had to admire the breadth of his wide shoulders, the strength in the muscles straining the fabric of his jeans. His hair had grown since his arrival, and dark tendrils brushed the collar of his denim jacket in the back. There was so much power in Jack Hunter, but there was tenderness, too. So much tenderness.

When she felt the back of her head she found the evidence of his careful ministrations. A sterile gauze bandage covered a very nasty bump. The scratches and scrapes on her face and hands had been washed and treated with bacterial cream. Jack had removed her boots and dirty clothes and changed her into a clean flannel shirt—his own, judging from the size and woodsy smell of it.

It was nice not to have to do anything. Always intent on proving her self-sufficiency, she'd never stopped to consider how comforting it was to be taken care of. The moment was so peaceful that she lay there a little longer and gave free rein to her thoughts.

Jack had responded well in the crisis, as well as a seasoned outdoorsman. That fact both elated and saddened her.

His accomplishment meant she'd been successful teaching him, but it also reminded her that her job was nearly over. In a few days he'd have no further need of her and would go back to Denver to pick up his life where he'd left it nearly a month ago. A life that had no place in it for her.

But she couldn't go on so easily. She would never be the same now that she'd known Jack. She'd miss him terribly, and she had no idea how she would fill the emptiness his leaving would bring.

"Jack?" she called softly.

He whirled around, a look of relief on his face. He was at her side immediately.

"Thank God you're awake. I was getting anxious."

When she sat up, a sliver of pain sliced through her head. "I've never had a serious hangover, but this must be what one feels like," she moaned.

He went to his pack and came back with a couple of aspirin tablets and a tin mug of water. "Take these. I kept checking you for signs of shock, but you seemed to be resting peacefully."

"I don't think there's any permanent damage," she concurred.

"I feel so responsible for what happened. Can you ever forgive me, Tess?"

"There's nothing to forgive. It was an accident, that's all." She looked around the tidy camp approvingly. "You have things well in hand here."

He grinned. "I was so worried about you I was operating on automatic pilot."

"You learned well."

"I had a good teacher. Do you want some stew? It's that deep-space dehydrated stuff, but it smells pretty good."

"Maybe later. I'm proud of the way you handled the situation, Jack. You did everything right by the book. I hadn't planned to provide such a realistic test of your rescue and first aid skills. You score A plus on all subjects."

He raked a hand through his hair, a gesture she was becoming familiar with and one she found particularly endearing. "I was horrified when I saw you fall. I felt so helpless, so powerless. I thought I'd lost you, and I couldn't bear it."

Tess smoothed her finger down his rough cheek. He hadn't shaved on the trail, and the dark shadow on his face only added to his rugged appeal. "But you weren't helpless. You knew what had to be done and you did it. I doubt I would have lasted long on that ledge alone. Your quick action probably saved my life.''

''Some cultures believe that when you save a life, it belongs to you,'' he said in a husky tone. ''That the two are inextricably entwined forever.''

Tess looked deeply into Jack's dark eyes in an attempt to fathom the meaning of his words. The raw emotion she saw mirrored there startled and unnerved her.

''I've never been much on superstitions,'' she said uneasily, more unsure than ever.

He turned away to stare into the fire. He still didn't know how to tell her everything he felt in his heart. He'd been so concerned about her well-being that he hadn't taken time to order his thoughts.

He'd planned to talk to her tonight, when they'd reached their destination. But since the accident the timing seemed inappropriate, and he didn't want her to think he was taking advantage of the situation.

''I think I'll have some of that stew now,'' she said quietly.

Thankful for something to do, Jack fixed her a plate and put water on to heat for hot chocolate. Now that darkness had drawn close there was an extra bite in the air.

''It'll be cold tonight,'' he observed.

''Which brings us to a problem. With my pack lost, we only have one sleeping bag between us.''

That wasn't the only thing between them, but he refrained from mentioning that fact. ''Yeah, I thought of that. There doesn't look to be much chance of rain, so we probably won't need a shelter. We can spread my tarp on the ground and use the unzipped sleeping bag as a cover. It won't be very soft, but it should be warm."

Especially if they shared their body heat. Jack hoped his willpower was in full working order tonight. He'd need it.

"That's a good idea," she said. "I'll clear away a spot for the tarp."

"Oh no you don't. You stay right where you are and eat your stew. I'll do it."

"I can help," she insisted.

"No," he said emphatically. "I'm going to be the hero this time."

Tess smiled. Maybe there was a good reason this damsel-in-distress thing had served so many generations of females.

She watched as Jack cleared small stones and debris out of an area near the fire. When he was satisfied, he picked up a flashlight and the tarp and disappeared in the darkness.

He came back a few minutes later and dumped a load of pine needles in the cleared spot, then spread the tarp over them. "It won't exactly be a feather bed, but it should be better than the bare ground," he told her as he worked.

After they finished eating, he put away their few dishes, hung his pack in a tree so wild animals wouldn't be tempted into their camp. As he banked the fire, he said, "We'll stay here tomorrow so you can rest before we head back to the lodge."

"I'm sorry we won't make it to the top of Mount McIver after all."

"There'll be other times for that," he assured her. He also reminded himself there would be plenty of time to talk about their future.

Will there, Jack? she wanted to ask. Will there really be another chance for us? How she wanted to believe that.

He stood and stretched. They'd put off the inevitable long enough. "We'd better turn in."

Tess unzipped the sleeping bag and spread it over the tarp. It was big enough that the two of them wouldn't have to huddle together beneath it. She made herself as comfortable as possible, and Jack eased in beside her, his big body immediately giving off an amazing amount of heat.

They were quiet for a time, each careful of arms and legs that might invade the other's space. An owl hooted in a distant tree, and the night air was thick with insect sounds.

"It sure is dark out here," he said. "When you live in the city with its car lights and street lamps and electrical excess, you forget what dark really is."

"It isn't so dark," Tess said with a smile. "There's the stars and the moon. In summer there are fireflies, and in winter there's snow, which has a glow all its own. I guess in the city the dark can be dangerous, but it's never seemed that way to me."

"Have you never wanted to see another part of the world, Tess?"

"No, I've always been satisfied where I am. I guess that shows a complete lack of curiosity and imagination on my part, doesn't it?"

"Not at all. I think it shows innate happiness."

Tess was pleased by his observation and turned toward him, resting her hand and chin on his shoulder. "Happiness can be elusive sometimes." After a few moments she added, "I'm glad you know about Greg Dexter."

"I'm sorry I went behind your back, but I had to know."

"I understand why you did that now. I should have told you myself. You've been so open the way you've shared your life with me. But I was so ashamed of what happened. I didn't want you to think I was a fool."

He cupped her face in his big hand. They were only inches apart but it was so dark he couldn't see her clearly. "I could never think that, Tess. Dexter was a cheat and a liar and a crook. You don't have to be ashamed of being his victim."

"Have you ever been a victim, Jack? If you haven't, you can't know how degrading it can be. In my mind I know it wasn't my fault, but I still blame myself for falling for his con. We almost lost everything because I let a stupid infatuation become too important to me. I was so selfish."

"But you didn't lose the lodge. You suffered and you learned and now you're wiser for it. That's what life is, Tess. A series of lessons. The survivors forgive and go on."

"I know. I'm trying to remember that."

"Don't remember. Forget." He gathered her in his arms and tugged her close. "Let me help you forget, Tess."

She wanted to lose herself in him, but there was folly in such abandon. She'd trusted before, and that trust had been betrayed and used against her. Would the hurt never go away? Would the past never give up its stranglehold on her emotions? "We shouldn't do this, Jack. It's too risky."

"You've taught me to take risks, Tess." With a smile in his voice, he added, "And I've learned to enjoy them."

He found her mouth in the darkness and kissed her hard. The restraint he'd counted on vanished when their lips touched. A fierce need for her surged through him, firing him, filling him, charging him with awareness of the soft woman he held.

Tess trembled in his arms and sought his comforting warmth. She worked her hand under his shirt and caressed the smoothly bunched muscles of his chest. Her finger slowly circled his male nipples and she felt him harden and tense against her. He wouldn't stop this time; he couldn't. And God help her, she didn't want him to.

He moaned her name over and over. The hungry litany touched her soul, and she opened herself up to him, ready to give, eager to receive. She clasped the back of his head to increase the pressure of his kiss and surrendered to the reckless desire that drove all other thoughts from her mind.

She wouldn't consider tomorrow, or the next day, or the day when Jack left for good. She wouldn't contemplate a future without him.

She would concentrate only on this moment, this night. This man.

Jack savored the kiss and cupped her breasts reverently in his hands. He stroked and caressed and massaged her, touching all the yearning places of her. He encouraged her explorations, and his flesh strained toward hers. A part of him knew that this was not the sequence of events as he had planned them and he struggled with his rioting emotions.

Before he loved her body, he had to be sure that she knew he loved her. All of her. And he had to know that she loved him in return.

He caught her questing hands in his and drew gently away from her lips. He held her close. His heart pounded, his breathing was labored and his willpower was shattered.

''I'm probably going to do this all wrong, Tess, but there is something I have to say before anything else happens between us.''

She stiffened, and the old doubts came back to make her wary. Here it comes, she thought. The moment of reckoning. The disclaimer. The rejection. She couldn't bear to hear it. Not from Jack.

''Save your breath, Hunter. I don't need the speech and I don't need you.'' She pushed away from him and straightened her clothes.

Her words were like cold stones, and Jack recoiled as if they'd struck him. What did she mean, she didn't need the speech? She didn't need him? Did she mean she didn't love him?

He'd done everything within his power to win her trust, and still she was ready to jump to all the wrong conclusions. He'd been a fool to think he could mend her ravaged heart. Her bitterness was like a sharp stick with which she kept the wound open.

Bitterness and pride. It was a terrible, consuming combination, and Tess McIver had nurtured hers far too long for tentative gestures to have any effect. She wasn't the only one with pride, but if they were to have any chance at happiness, Jack knew he would have to swallow his. He would have to tell her his feelings because it hurt too much to hold them inside.

"I love you, Tess." The words were wrenched from him.

She gasped at the unexpected declaration. "I didn't expect you to say—"

"Be quiet and listen to me. I know it's happened fast. A month isn't supposed to be long enough for two people to really get to know each other's hearts and minds. But considering the circumstances and all we've been through together, we can't consider ourselves typical."

"Jack—"

He was determined to talk now that he'd made a start, and he paid her no heed. He'd say this. And she would listen.

"I know we have a lot to overcome. A lot of very basic differences that will complicate things no end. But those same differences will also make life interesting and exciting."

"I—"

He interrupted her. "You've focused only on the negative things, but we're alike in ways you haven't even considered. Maybe we don't have the same backgrounds or experiences, but our reactions to life have been remarkably similar. We've both made mistakes and we've overcompensated for our pain.

"You, by shutting yourself away from the world, and me, by making myself a public figure. I've come to know you well, Tess. I understand you in a way no other man can. Every human being needs a special person to share his life. You are the person I need, and I believe with all my heart that I am the person you need."

"Jack!" This time she succeeded in getting his attention. "What are you talking about?"

"Us, dammit! You and me. Together forever, happily ever after. I want you to marry me, Tess."

"Whaat?" She was so surprised by his heartfelt words that she could only stammer.

"Wait a minute. Before you answer that, answer another question. Do you love me?"

"Jack, this is crazy," she said, grinning.

"I know." He laughed. "Do you love me, Tess?"

"Yes. Yes, yes. Yes—" His lips silenced her and their mutual need eclipsed everything else. Jack was right. He understood her so well, but she'd been afraid to admit it before.

"That's all I need to know." He rolled onto his back and stared up at the starry canopy above. God, could it be so simple? All the hours he'd spent working out the details. Planning, plotting, picturing the life they would forge together. Could it really be so easily resolved?

Tess snuggled against him, happier than she'd ever been in her life. She loved Jack and he loved her. What that meant in terms of the future, she couldn't attempt to understand at this moment. For now it was enough to know her love was returned.

He sat up suddenly and grasped her shoulders. "You didn't answer my first question. Will you marry me, Tess?"

He made her dizzy, just as she had been when she'd teetered on the edge of the cliff. A wrong move could prove fatal. Marriage? Love was one thing, one big thing to be sure, and it would take her a while just to assimilate the enormity of it.

But marriage? That was the most important commitment two people could ever make. How did anyone have the courage to do it?

"I know it seems like a big step," he pressed. "But I've given this a lot of thought and I think I have everything figured out."

"I don't know, Jack."

He looked wounded. "I thought you said you loved me."

"I do. More than I ever thought I could love anyone. But I'm not sure marriage would work for us. For me."

He moved away from her. This was not how it had happened in his plans. Like a child whistling in the dark, he'd made allowances for the fact that Tess might not love him. But never had it occurred to him that she could share his feelings and not want the permanence of marriage.

"And why not?"

"Your life is in Denver. You have a job and commitments there. I live in these mountains. It's the only world I've ever known or wanted. I can't give it up."

He kissed her again and relief was apparent in his words. "Is that all it is?"

"You don't understand."

"Yes, I do. I'm not asking you to give up your way of life, I want to share it with you. If things go like I planned, I'll be free to be with you at Big Bear. Bitterroot and I have discussed this already, and I have a plan to bail the lodge out of trouble. I have money to invest and we can use it to turn the lodge around. We can be partners, Tess. In every sense of the word."

Tess listened, but it wasn't Jack's words she heard. It was Greg's.

With a sickening sense of déjà vu, she recalled how another man had made the same promises. And how he had broken them. She panicked, and her fear made her crueler than she wanted to be. "Jack, don't. I've heard all that before. Do you think I'm fool enough to fall for the same line twice?"

He stared at her, uncomprehendingly. The moon had risen as they talked, and its pale glow illuminated her face. But he could not read the emotions there.

"You can't mean to compare me to Dexter." The anguish in his words tore at her resolve.

Tess chided herself. This was Jack talking, not Greg. Jack was good and kind and funny and dear. Jack had never done anything to hurt her. Greg was the liar, the giver of pain.

"No, of course not. I'm sorry. I guess I'm not really over it. I may never be. Don't push me on this, Jack. Give me time."

But Jack didn't have time. The wheels had already been set in motion. He'd staked his career, his reputation, his whole future, on his ability to heal Tess's heart. If he failed ...

He heard the sound of her weeping and gathered her into his arms. "Don't cry. We'll work this out. You'll see," he told her.

"I'm scared, Jack. More scared than I've ever been." She loved him, but she feared being able to give that love completely now. She wanted to let down her defenses, to trust him in this as she'd trusted him after the accident. She'd given herself into his keeping then, why couldn't she do so now?

Jack was hurt by her reticence, but he knew how deep the scars went and he refused to give up hope.

"Just let me hold you," he whispered.

She relaxed in his arms and they lay side by side under a brilliant night sky pierced by a million cold stars.

Chapter Eleven

The next morning Tess announced that she did not need further rest. "I've recovered my strength and I'm ready to return to the lodge."

"If you're sure." Jack was wounded by her apparent eagerness to escape his company, and feared what it might mean. As he packed up their belongings, he took care to leave the primitive campsite as they'd found it.

They scattered the dead ashes from the fire and returned the fire-pit rocks to their original sites. He put the pine needles back under the trees. When they were finished, the place was cleaner and wilder than when they'd arrived.

They would have to spend one more night on the trail before they reached the lodge. One more night in which words of longing would be left unspoken. One more night in which desire would go unfulfilled.

Jack slowed his pace to accommodate Tess, but because she was not burdened with a pack, she had no trouble keeping up. By unspoken agreement, he unerringly led the way and Tess followed, free to ponder all that had happened. This trip had been far more than a test of Jack's outdoor skills. It had been a decisive turning point in their lives.

He had offered her love and marriage and security. A package deal. Her refusal had hurt him immeasurably. She, better than anyone, knew how painful rejection could be. Still undecided, she wondered if she would yet have a chance to make things right between them, or would his stoic silence carry him back to Denver and out of her life forever?

That night when they camped, Jack was careful to avoid subjects that might make Tess feel pressured. He reminisced about his time at the lodge. He talked about the harrowing drive to the hospital after he shot himself, and confessed that he'd envied her cool capability.

"I thought you were the biggest fool I'd ever met," she admitted with a laugh. "It made me furious that I also found you maddeningly attractive."

"Do you still think I'm a fool?" he asked.

"No."

"Do you still find me attractive?"

"Oh, yes," she answered against his lips, for their bodies could not exercise the judgment of their minds, and the need between them only made their situation more painful.

Jack sensed that Tess wanted to make love to him. But for the first time in his life, that wasn't enough. So he asked no more than her comforting nearness. They spent the night in each other's arms, her doubts like a wall between them.

They reached the lodge early the next afternoon. Bitterroot was on hand to greet them and, surprisingly enough, so was Maddie Flame. The older couple asked questions about the trip and listened intently as Jack and Tess related the details of the accident.

Once Bitterroot assured himself that his daughter was all right, he exchanged uneasy glances with Maddie.

"What's going on here?" Tess asked her father. "It's as plain as red paint that you two have something on your minds."

"Well, now we didn't want to spring nothin' on you sudden like, but there's someone here to see you, Jack," Bitterroot said.

Jack raised a brow questioningly, and Bitterroot gave him a meaningful look. At that moment the door opened and a man came in and enclosed Jack in a bear hug.

"You did it," he said as he thrust a copy of the *Denver Post* into Jack's hands. "I can't believe it, but it worked out just like you said it would."

The man was half a foot shorter than Jack, but there was strength in his wiry build. He had a thinning thatch of sandy-blond hair and a happy, likable face.

"You must be Tess. I'd know you anywhere." He gave her a hug and a brotherly kiss on the cheek. "Congratulations to you both."

Tess looked to Jack for a clue to the stranger's identity. "Jack, why don't you introduce me to your friend."

Jack was so busy trying to absorb everything, that he was slow with the amenities.

"I'm Norton Greene," the man introduced himself. "And I'm the closest thing this big lug has to a brother, so I'm going to think of you as my sister. I hope that's all right with you, Tess."

"Fine." She wondered if she sounded as bewildered as she felt. "Jack, what's going on?"

"I'm not sure," Jack said, clearly as frustrated as she. He turned to his friend. "Norton, what are you doing here?"

Norton looked confused and hurt, like a child who's just learned he wasn't invited to the party. "I came because you're my best friend, and I wanted to give the good news in person."

"What good news?" Tess demanded.

Norton retrieved the paper from Jack and unfolded it to a page he obviously knew well. The Sunday edition of the *Post* had a much-read appearance.

"What?" Tess exclaimed.

Jack snatched the paper out of her hands before she could do much more than scan the headline in question. It read *Hunter At Large* Canceled.

"I think you and I need to have a little talk first, Nort. In private."

"No, I think we should all have a little talk. Together." Tess didn't know what was going on, but everyone's cryptic behavior was most curious.

"Oh, dear," Maddie wailed. "Tess doesn't seem too happy about all this, does she?"

Bitterroot tugged on her arm. "I think we should fix a little snack for everyone. What do you say, Maddie?"

"Oh, yes," she agreed. "Refreshments, that's what we need." They scurried out of the room.

"Okay, Jack," Tess demanded. "What is this about your show being canceled?"

"Canceled?" he asked in mock surprise. "Let me see that paper."

"If your show has been canceled, prematurely ending your television career, why is your best friend, who is the closest thing you have to a brother, so damned happy about it?"

"Well, it's simple, really." Jack's nimble mind had never failed him before and he hoped it wouldn't do so now.

"Good. I'd like a simple explanation."

"Should I leave?" Norton asked.

"No, you should stay," she told him. "Somehow I get the feeling you know more about this than either one of us." With that she yanked the paper back and quickly read the article. She looked up at Jack in alarm.

"It says here that *Hunter At Large* was canceled after the producers discovered its host was a fraud. It says the *Post* ran an article about your lack of outdoors skill after an anonymous caller leaked the details to a staff reporter."

"Really?" Jack pretended to read the article over Tess's shoulder. "It says all that, huh?"

"Yes, it does. Now, what I want to know is why is that good news?" Jack only smiled sheepishly, so she turned her fierce glare on Norton. "Why don't you explain all this to me?"

Norton nudged Jack in the ribs with his elbow. "You mean she doesn't know yet?"

Jack gave his friend a dirty look.

"No! I do not know yet," she answered in a deadly voice. "Clue me in, Norton."

Jack nodded. "Go ahead, pal."

Norton demurred. "I think I'll take a walk down by the cove. It's all yours, buddy."

"Coward," Jack called after him. "Some friend you turned out to be."

"Dammit, Jack. What is going on?"

"It's simple, really."

"You keep saying that."

"I'm not sure where I should begin."

"Try the beginning."

He groaned. How could he tell Tess everything? He'd taken so much for granted. Assumed more than he should have. They were supposed to return to the lodge after the hike with a wedding day all picked out.

God, how was he going to explain what he'd done in light of her refusal to marry him? He'd look like such a fool.

"Jack," she prompted.

"Oh, all right. I thought you would agree to marry me."

"That's it? That's your explanation?"

"Not really, but it all sounds kind of silly now that you've turned me down. Oh, I knew you'd have reservations all right. That's why I wanted to have all the details worked out before I asked you. I wanted to be able to show you what kind of life we'd have together.''

''I still don't understand.''

''I know.'' He raked back his hair. ''I knew I couldn't ask you to give up Big Bear and move to Denver to be with me. You belong here. These mountains are a part of you, a part that I love, I might add. I knew that if we were to be together, I'd have to stay here—''

''You were willing to give up your way of life and your career to stay here?'' she asked incredulously.

''Not exactly,'' he stressed.

''Tell me.''

''I wouldn't be giving up anything that was important to me. I never really felt comfortable hosting that show, and I had no career ambitions in that direction. Norton is the one who really deserves all the credit for making the program a success, and after you and I talked about changing the focus of the program, I figured it would be a chance for him to replace me. So I set the wheels in motion.''

''When?'' she asked softly. ''How?''

''The night we went to Vail for the pizza, I called Marcia Murphy and told her I wanted out.''

''You did?''

''Yeah.''

''What did she say?''

''She laughed and reminded me that my contract had two more years to run and there was no way she'd let me out.''

Tess tried to comprehend what he was saying. "What happened then?"

"I figured that if they wouldn't release me, I'd just have to make sure they fired me. Norton tried to talk me out of it, but Maddie's article gave me an idea. If the public learned I was a fraud, they'd have to let me go."

"But the producers knew all about that already," Tess said. "The whole thing was their idea in the first place."

"I know. But television stations don't like to look foolish. They needed an out. So I simply gave them one."

"You were the anonymous caller," she accused.

He only grinned and shrugged. "It was a dirty job, but somebody had to do it."

"Why is Norton so happy? Isn't he out of a job now, too?"

"Nope. We figured Marcia would have to do something when *Hunter At Large* was canceled or risk being out on her ear. So she came up with an idea for a new show. Its focus will be on camping and hiking and survival skills. It will feature campground critiques and family vacation spots."

"But that was *your* idea," she protested.

He smiled like a Cheshire cat. "Yep. It was a pretty darn good one, too. In all her brilliance, Marcia decided that likable, trustworthy Norton would be perfect for a family show and hired him to host *Greene Country*. Nort's finally going to get the credit he deserves."

"And Marcia Murphy gets the credit she doesn't deserve," Tess observed sourly.

"Hey," Jack said with a grin. "That's show biz."

Before Tess could reply, she heard the roar of engines outside. She threw up her arms. "Now what?"

They stepped outside and saw a caravan of trucks chugging up the mountain road that served as Big Bear's driveway. They pulled onto the grounds of the lodge and switched off their engines. The burly driver of the lead truck jumped out of the cab and sauntered up to the couple on the porch.

"You Hunter or McIver?" he barked.

"I'm Jack Hunter. This is Tess McIver."

"Where do you want this stuff unloaded?"

"What stuff?" Tess made no attempt to hide her frustration. "Will somebody kindly tell me what is going on?"

"I thought you and McIver were partners." The driver eyed Jack skeptically.

"We are. That is, we will be. Her father is my partner too and . . . let me show you where to unload."

Jack took charge and the drivers began emptying the trucks of cargo: lumber, building supplies, appliances, furniture and fixtures. Everything they needed to restore the lodge to its former glory. And then some.

Bitterroot and Maddie came out, and the old man took over from Jack. "See, Tess. Everything's worked out just fine," he said before he left to direct the truckers.

"Am I crazy or is everybody else?" Tess wailed.

Jack wrapped his arms around her.

"We're both a little crazy. People in love always are. I learned a lot of lessons from you, Tess McIver," he said in a husky voice. "You taught me to take risks, and you taught me that actions speak louder than words. I knew it wouldn't be enough for me just to tell you I loved you and wanted to spend the rest of my life here with you . . ."

"So you decided to show me," she finished for him.

"I want to help you rebuild the lodge. I want it to be the place your great-grandfather envisioned. I love you, Tess, and I want to raise our children here in this clean, unspoiled world of yours. This world of ours, if you'll have me."

"But Jack, can you really be happy stuck way up here in total obscurity? With no bright lights and no real job?"

"I can be happy wherever you are. And as for a job, I plan to be the third best wilderness guide in Colorado, with your help. I also have plans to write the great American novel. I'll need lots of solitude for that."

He looked so happy and optimistic that Tess threw her arms around his neck. "Jack, I love you. I'm sorry I let my foolish pride stand between us."

"Do you trust me, Tess?"

"Yes," she said, gazing into his eyes. "Can you ever forgive me?"

"I can only love you, Tess. Forever."

Bitterroot and Maddie watched the lovers with tears in their eyes. Norton returned from his walk and beamed with the knowledge that he would soon be called on to be the best man at a wedding. Even the tough truckers stopped in their tasks to gaze longingly at the two on the porch.

Jack held Tess, and the power of his love dissolved the last of her doubts, made all the risks worthwhile. There was so much more she wanted to tell him, if only his questing lips would let her speak.

She smiled happily and returned the kiss. They had the rest of their long, long lives to talk.

* * * * *

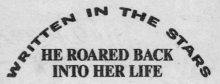

Silhouette Special Edition

proudly hails

WOMEN OF GLORY

from Lindsay McKenna

Soar with Dana Coulter, Molly Rutledge and Maggie Donovan—Lindsay McKenna's WOMEN OF GLORY. On land, sea or air, these three Annapolis grads challenge danger head-on, risking life and limb for the glory of their country—and for the men they love!

May: NO QUARTER GIVEN (SE #667) Dana Coulter is on the brink of achieving her lifelong dream of flying—and of meeting the man who would love to take her to new heights!

June: THE GAUNTLET (SE #673) Molly Rutledge is determined to excel on her own merit, but Captain Cameron Sinclair is equally determined to take gentle Molly under his wing....

July: UNDER FIRE (SE #679) Indomitable Maggie never thought her career—or her heart—would come under fire. But all that changes when she teams up with Lieutenant Wes Bishop!

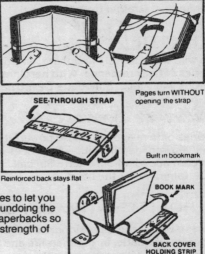

FOUR UNIQUE SERIES
FOR EVERY WOMAN YOU ARE...

Silhouette Romance®

Tender, delightful, provocative—stories that capture the laughter, the tears, the *joy* of falling in love. Pure romance...straight from the heart!

SILHOUETTE *Desire*®

Go wild with Desire! Passionate, emotional, sensuous stories of fiery romance. With heroines you'll like and heroes you'll *love*, Silhouette Desire never fails to deliver.

Silhouette Special Edition®

Stories of love and life, these powerful novels are tales that you can identify with—romances with "something special" added in! Silhouette Special Edition is entertainment for the heart.

SILHOUETTE·INTIMATE·MOMENTS™

Enter a world where passions run hot and excitement is the rule. Dramatic, larger-than-life and always compelling—Silhouette Intimate Moments will never let you down.